UNTIL WE MEET AGAIN

ROBERTA KAGAN

Storm

Ebook ISBN: 978-1-80508-721-2
Paperback ISBN: 978-1-80508-723-6

Cover design: Debbie Clement
Cover images: Shutterstock, Trevillion

Published by Storm Publishing.
For further information, visit:
www.stormpublishing.co

ALSO BY ROBERTA KAGAN

Margot's Secret

The Secret They Hid

An Innocent Child

Margot's Secret

The Blood Sisters

The Pact

My Sister's Betrayal

When Forever Ends

The Auschwitz Twins

The Children's Dream

Mengele's Apprentice

The Auschwitz Twins

Jews, The Third Reich, and a Web of Secrets

My Son's Secret

The Stolen Child

A Web of Secrets

All My Love, Detrick

All My Love, Detrick

You Are My Sunshine

The Promised Land

To Be An Israeli

Forever, My Homeland

A Nazi On Trial In God's Court

The Heart Of A Gypsy

The Gypsy Witch

A Time Of Anarchy

One Last Hope

PROLOGUE

Chloe Levin would not let him see her cry. She was terrified of him, but he would never know it.

They stood outside the administration building at Auschwitz.

"Dance for me, ballerina," the SS officer commanded, eyeing her up and down. Her stomach turned.

"Not on your life." Chloe spat the words out.

He laughed. "Have you ever heard the term 'Burn, Witch, Burn!'? Well, if you keep this up, that might just be your fate."

"That's your plan, isn't it? That's what you do to all Jews," Chloe replied sharply, trying to keep her voice even.

"That remains to be seen."

Another Nazi officer walked over, glanced at Chloe, and then turned to the SS officer. "I'll take this from here."

"Be careful, Ostendorff. You show far too much sensitivity towards these Jews. If you keep it up, it might cost you your career."

Ostendorff glared at him. "I am your superior officer. If you speak that way to me again, it could cost you your life."

ONE

1925

Chloe Levin sat down at a table in the back of a small and inexpensive restaurant with greasy tablecloths and mismatched silverware. Her hands trembled as she clutched her handbag. She was worried about spending her francs in case Lily, her daughter, wrote to her from America and needed financial help.

One of the girls who worked on the factory line with Chloe hadn't shown up for work that morning. This slowed down production and meant that Chloe had to stay at work until late. On her way home, Chloe had stopped at a small café to get something to eat. This was unusual for her because she saved every penny she could. But tonight she was too tired to try and find a store that remained open so she could go shopping for food. Still, she knew she must eat.

Chloe's eyes scanned the menu for the least expensive option when fortune intervened. Sensing someone watching her, she looked up to see a well-dressed man at least ten years her senior standing beside her table. Although he was not conventionally handsome, he was pleasant to look at. He was tall and well-built, and unlike most men of his age, his hair had not yet turned gray; it was still dark and very thick.

"Is it possible?" he asked, his eyes dancing with delight.

She looked up from the menu she was reading. "I'm sorry? I don't know what you are talking about."

"Are you Chloe Mandel-Levin?"

Surprised that this stranger knew her name, she put the menu down. "How do you know who I am?" she asked.

"You are a celebrity, my dear. It's so wonderful to meet you. My name is Maurice Lambert," he said excitedly. "I saw you dance when you were just a child and I've followed your career. I was heartbroken when you married Maximilian Levin and stopped dancing."

"My goodness. I had no idea that anyone even noticed me when I was a ballerina, or if they did, I didn't think they would remember me after so many years." Chloe felt a flush of pride creeping up her neck.

"I remember." The man smiled warmly, and his gaze drifted to the tattered sleeve of her dress. She tried to hide it, but he looked away so quickly that she wondered if she had imagined him seeing it. "Please, won't you allow me to buy you dinner?"

"Oh, that's really not necessary," Chloe said, her hands self-consciously covering her sleeve.

"It would be my honor," he replied. "Won't you please allow me this indulgence?"

He was so chivalrous, and Chloe was hungry. She might have been able to afford some bread and warm milk but nothing more. "Thank you," she said. "Won't you please sit down?"

"We would be squeezed in at this small table and I believe that a meal should be a lovely experience. Don't you agree?" he asked.

"Yes, I do." Chloe stood up and smiled as he escorted her to a larger table. She fumbled with the menu; she was unsure what to order because he was paying the bill and that made her uncomfortable.

Noticing her unease, he asked, "Do you like *boeuf bourguignon*? I've had it here before and it's quite good."

"I do actually," she replied, embarrassed as her stomach growled.

"May I order for you?" he asked.

"Please."

He ordered the stew along with a crisp green salad and two glasses of red wine. While they waited for their food, he said, "I know you are no longer dancing. However, would you ever consider teaching ballet to youngsters? I own a studio and, well... just having your name listed as my top instructor would be quite a draw for young students."

"I don't know if I could," she said honestly even though the idea of working at a dance studio excited her. "I've never taught before."

"I think you would be wonderful at it," he said gently.

"Do you really?"

"I do. In fact, I'll pay you well if you'll consider my offer."

Chloe felt her heart flip; she couldn't let this opportunity pass her by. "I'll do it."

"Good. Can you start on tomorrow?"

"Yes, I can."

"That's wonderful news. Let's enjoy our meal and when we've finished eating, I'll give you the address of the studio."

TWO

Chloe went home that evening and thought about her conversation with Maurice. She took off her coat and put her handbag on the chair of the small table in her humble apartment. Then she walked over to her mirror and studied herself. As she twirled her long flaxen hair around her finger, her aqua-blue eyes sparkled. Then she turned to the side and admired her still-slim dancer's figure and smiled. *I haven't danced in years, but I still have the frame and flexibility*, she thought.

She remembered moving back to Paris a few years ago. No one she met could believe she was middle-aged; most people mistook her for someone in their late twenties. Chloe filled the kettle with water and placed it on the burner. Leaving it to warm up, she went to change into her sleepwear before returning to the kitchen and sitting down at the table.

Ahh, it's been so many years since I've been in a dance studio, she reflected. *I hope I haven't bitten off more than I can chew, but I want this so badly.*

The thought of dancing again brought such joy to Chloe, and she hadn't felt joy since her daughter, Lily, left with her husband and baby for America. Lily imagined herself dancing and memories of the studio in Paris flooded her mind... *I was so young. I had so many hopes and dreams. I was sure that I was destined to be a prima ballerina. I was in love with dancing and with Paris, but God had other plans and then I met Max. Oh, Max.* Chloe sighed aloud. *I miss you so much, my love.*

Chloe thought of Max walking through the door in his military uniform. *I remember the day you came home like it was yesterday. I have never been so happy in my life. To be wrapped in your arms again, to breathe in your aroma, the way your lips felt pressed against mine.* She reached up and touched her lips. Just then the tea kettle started to whistle, bringing Chloe back to the present moment. She stood up, poured herself a cup of boiling water, and added the last tea bag from her cupboard. Her bare shelves reminded Chloe of her financial troubles. *I hope this job with Maurice works out,* she thought desperately. *Leaving the factory is such a risk, but it's a horrible working environment, and I hardly make enough money to live.* As the tea brewed, she lost herself in memories of Max and their lives in Germany after the Great War.

Chloe finished her tea. *I wonder if Max is right. Will Lily and Mimi come home to me one day? Will we all live in Paris together?* She yawned and stretched her arms out. *I need to get some sleep,* she thought. *Tomorrow is a big day. My first time back in a dance studio in so many years. I really hope I still have the ability to do this.* She looked up at the ceiling of her apartment. *Max, please send me the strength and guidance I need to make this work.*

THREE

Chloe's career as a dance teacher began the next morning. With the money from her first pay envelope, she rented a room in a building for women near the dance studio and furnished it with used furniture from a local thrift store. She found plants in the trash and carefully nursed them back to health. She hung her few precious paintings on the walls and made drapes out of old sheets for the windows. By the time she finished, her apartment had an eclectic charm.

Most of Chloe's students were twelve- and thirteen-year-olds who shared the same dreams: they all yearned to be prima ballerinas as Chloe once had. Sharing her love for ballet with others who felt the same fulfilled and rejuvenated her. All the dance exercises she had learned as a student came flooding back as she looked at the hopeful faces of the young women at the studio.

It was impossible for Chloe not to care deeply about her ambitious students, and they adored her. Most of them worked very hard, and Chloe often stayed after class to bandage their bleeding feet. Their dedication reminded her of her student days when she had practiced for so many hours at a time that it consumed her. That was how she had injured herself.

Chloe had been practicing her drop lift on that awful day. The lift followed a long sequence and finished with a flying split leap. She had been working all night, and her body was growing tired. But she vowed that she would stick the landing just once before allowing herself to retire for the evening, and she was so close. She set herself up to begin the sequence one last time, perfecting every move before she came to the final leap. She took off, but something distracted her midair and she lost her focus. When Chloe hit the floor, she landed badly and injured her ankle. This experience had taught her the pain of trying too hard, and she attempted to talk to her students about moderation. They didn't listen, just as she wouldn't have listened to such advice before her accident derailed her dancing career.

At least twice a week, Chloe stayed long past the time when the studio closed, trying to help a student. Chloe's desire to help these girls knew no boundaries; she often worked with a young dancer who was scheduled to go to an audition for hours on end. Maurice could see that Chloe was devoted to her students and to his studio, and he often gave her financial bonuses to show his appreciation. For Chloe, the most difficult part of being a ballet teacher was knowing that most of her students would never realize their dreams. Most would fall short and be forced to find a way to live their lives without ever dancing professionally.

Chloe quickly learned that her first impression, that Maurice might want to be her lover, was wrong. He was not romantically interested in her as he was openly homosexual. Men found him irresistible and his lovers were numerous. Women found him irresistible, too, but he always gently and kindly refused their attentions.

Her professional relationship with Maurice soon blossomed into best friendship. He was very generous and often paid for tickets so they might attend the ballet, theater, or opera together. Chloe would feel like a princess on these special occasions. She would take her time getting ready, putting on her rouge and her finest dress. Maurice would pick her up at her apartment looking dashing, and the two of them would head to the theater. The energy of being in the audience was almost as electrifying as being on stage. As the lights dimmed, Chloe would find her heart racing as if she were about to perform. The ballets were beautiful and when Chloe found herself crying, Maurice would hand her his satin handkerchief to dab her tears. After the productions they would find a café with live music and after a few glasses of wine Maurice would spin Chloe around the dance floor with ease. They were both light-footed and graceful. Maurice was well known in Paris, loved by everyone for his kindness and generosity. He introduced Chloe to all his interesting friends: painters, sculptors, musicians, and authors who frequented local bars and restaurants.

One night, six months after Chloe had started working at Maurice's studio, she lay awake in bed. She missed her daughter, Lily, and her late husband, Max, terribly. She clutched the photograph of Max that sat on her bedside table to her chest as tears rolled down her cheeks. *After death, will Max and I be together again?* she wondered. The intensity of Chloe's longing to feel Max's arms around her was almost unbearable and she began to think about what it would feel like to die. *Will it be painful? What will lie on the other side of my last and final breath? Could it be Max? If death means we will be together again, then I am ready to leave this earth.*

But she heard Max's voice in her head. *Think of Lily and Mimi. What if they need you?*

Recalling her husband's gentle love for his family, Chloe challenged her instincts. *You must not even think of dying,* she told herself. *If you took your own life, Lily would never recover. She would blame herself for moving to America. At best, it would ruin Lily's marriage. At worst, it would ruin the rest of Lily's life. I am a mother before anything else; I am Lily's mother now and forever. My daughter must come first, before myself,* Chloe thought as she sighed aloud.

She couldn't sleep so she got out of bed and put on a simple gray dress and a pair of low-heeled black shoes. Chloe didn't bother with lipstick or mascara, she just grabbed her handbag and walked downstairs. Living in an apartment in a woman's building was sometimes difficult because she had an eleven o'clock curfew. It was already very late, and she knew she would be locked out if she didn't return on time. Looking up, she checked the clock. It was a little before ten o'clock. That left her an hour to go out for a walk.

The night air felt cool and fresh on Chloe's skin. For a moment she stood outside under the stars and closed her eyes. In her mind she could see Max's face; she remembered a night long ago when they had walked hand in hand under the Paris sky. She often spoke silently to Max on her evening walks, hoping that her thoughts reached him somehow. *I miss you so much, Max. I am happy at my job. In fact, I love it. My students mean so much to me. But no one can replace you. You were always the love of my life. I can still remember our first kiss.*

Chloe opened her eyes and realized that she was crying. She took an embroidered handkerchief out of her handbag and wiped hot tears from her cheeks. Then she looked at the handkerchief. Her mother had made it for her and presented it to her on her wedding day. *Oh Mama, I miss you, too*, she thought sadly. *I wish that those who we love could live forever.*

Chloe was not ready to return to her lonely apartment, so she kept walking. She passed a local café that was known as a gathering place for international artists and decided to go inside. She had been to this café a couple of times with Maurice, and always found it exciting. Chloe sat down at a table in the back of a semi-dark room and ordered a glass of white wine. She sipped the wine slowly and looked around the room. Men—some in suits, others more disheveled—sat together or with women. Most of the women were very stylish, wearing their hair bobbed. They were dressed in pants instead of skirts or dresses. The quirky artistic atmosphere made Chloe smile. It entertained her to listen to the couple who sat at the table next to her. They were arguing feverishly about schools of philosophy. Chloe had no idea what the word "existentialism" meant or who Nietzsche was, but she was fascinated by how passionately these two were engaged in their conversation. The woman noticed Chloe watching them and shot her a questioning look. Embarrassed by her own eavesdropping, Chloe looked away.

A tall young woman walked up to the front of the room where a piano waited. She sat down and began to play. Her voice was deep and raspy. Chloe closed her eyes and felt transported by the music. She didn't know the words to the song, but she found herself humming the melody.

"Can I get you something else?" a young waitress asked.

"Oh no, thank you," Chloe replied, opening her eyes and asking for the check.

The streets were quiet as Chloe left the café except for soft music wafting from a dance hall on the corner. As she turned the corner a couple walked past her arm in arm, and she was struck again with longing for Max.

FOUR

1926

The following winter was exceptionally cold. On a frigid morning a week after Valentine's Day, Chloe was on her way to the market to purchase food. It had snowed the night before and since she was outside very early the white powder blanket on the ground was not yet filled with gray slush or footprints.

Under the rays of the rising morning sun, the snow sparkled in rainbows like fairy dust from a children's fable. As Chloe walked through the city she marveled at the beauty of the snow-dusted Eiffel Tower. Two children wearing heavy coats, scarves, and hats were laughing as they built a snowman in front of Le Bon Marché.

Chloe watched them, thinking that they were outside very early. The children ran around laughing and hurling snowballs at each other. She closed her eyes and remembered how her life had been when Lily was that age. Then she thought about a letter she had recently received from Lily telling her all about Mimi, her granddaughter; it brought a pang of longing to her chest. Lily mentioned that she sang the same lullaby to Mimi that Chloe had always sung to her.

If I could make a wish, just one wish, it would be to see Mimi and Lily again, Chloe thought. *Joe tells Lily that they can't afford to come back to Paris, but maybe I can get a second job and earn enough money to take a boat to America.*

Chloe grabbed a pencil and paper from her bag and sat down on a bench to draw up a budget. She quickly realized that on her salary, even if she could withstand the rigors of a second job, it would be impossible to save enough to pay for even the cheapest passage. It was a hopeless plan, regardless of how frugal she was willing to be. She stood up from the bench and a cold gust of wind sent a chill through her entire body; Chloe wrapped her coat a little tighter around her body to keep the freezing air out and headed towards the market. She was lost in thoughts of her daughter and grandchild, and because she was so distracted she never noticed the patch of ice that was hidden by a drift of snow. When her foot hit the ice, she slipped and fell.

That was the first time she saw him. He had to be the most handsome man she had ever laid eyes on. The winter sun illuminated his head like a golden halo. He wore a black cashmere coat and had a dark gray cashmere scarf wrapped around his neck. When he got close enough for her to see his face clearly, she noticed that the most mesmerizing part of him was his eyes. They were a deep navy blue that almost appeared black. Chloe was so entranced by this attractive man that she forgot to be embarrassed that she was laying sprawled out on the ground on a sheet of ice. He walked briskly towards her, looking concerned. His French was very poor, and she was certain she detected a German accent, but he managed to say, "Are you alright, miss? May I help you get up?"

It was then that Chloe felt her face flush. She pulled her coat down to cover her exposed thigh. "Oh, yes please. I'm rather embarrassed."

"No need to be. It's cold and icy so it's only natural to slip." He put his arm around her waist and lifted her so gently that for a moment she couldn't feel his hand on her body. Once she was standing, he helped her to walk slowly off the ice before asking, "Are you hurt?"

Chloe could tell from his facial expressions as he tried to

communicate with her in French that he was struggling with the language.

She nodded. "I'm fine. Thank you. And... by the way, if it's easier for you, I speak fluent German. My late husband taught me. We spent some time in Germany during the Great War."

"Did you?" the man said and immediately switched to speaking in German. "This ice can be very tricky, I'm afraid. Are you quite sure you weren't hurt?"

"Yes, thank you. I really am fine." Chloe straightened her hair.

"My name is Rudolf, but you can call me Rudy."

"I'm Chloe."

"I know this is rather bold, but may I buy you a coffee or some breakfast perhaps?" he asked.

If I refuse, I might never see him again, Chloe realized. "I'd like that," she replied.

"Coffee or breakfast?" he asked earnestly.

"Why don't we go and have some breakfast?" she said, smiling.

"I happen to know that there's a sweet little café right around the corner. They make a delicious *croque madame*. They also have strong coffee. I could use one."

"Me too," she replied, rubbing her leg, which was starting to throb with pain, and dabbing at the graze on her knee with a tissue.

"I don't mean to overstep my boundaries, but it's very slippery out here. So, may I ask that you take my arm so I can escort you? I wouldn't want to risk you falling over again."

"Of course," Chloe said, taking his arm. "I really do appreciate your assistance." They walked for a short distance. The chilly wind felt like tiny fragments of ice on her face.

Rudy opened the door to the café and they entered. The owner, stood behind the counter, directed them to a table right in front of a large window. Like a gentleman he pulled out her chair. She had to admit that she found his old-fashioned manners charming. He helped Chloe to take off her coat and noticed that she had skinned her knee when she fell. "You're bleeding. Does it hurt?" he asked. Without waiting, he motioned the waiter to come to the table. "Before we order, please can we have a napkin and some warm water?"

The waiter nodded. "I'll bring them right away, sir."

"Oh, this is not necessary," Chloe said, suddenly embarrassed by all the attention.

"It is," he insisted kindly.

Once the waiter brought the water and the napkin, the man cleaned her injury carefully. "It doesn't look too bad now that it's cleaned up," he said gently.

She smiled as he sat down beside her. "Thank you again. I feel like all I'm doing today is constantly thanking you."

"If you're always thanking me for something, I'll know that I've done well and I've made my mother proud. She always insisted that my brother and I behave like gentlemen. Even though we were little ruffians as children." He laughed.

Chloe laughed, too.

Rudy ordered them both coffee and *croque madames*. They sat and enjoyed their warm drinks while Rudy told Chloe about his friends and their mischievous activities in *biergartens* during Oktoberfest. She laughed with him and even though she had never met his friends, she felt like she had known them for years.

When the food arrived, Chloe's stomach growled as she looked at her plate. Slices of ham and cheese oozed out from between two thick slices of grilled brioche bread. When she took her first bite, she forgot the throbbing pain in her knee.

At the end of the meal, Rudy paid the check and escorted Chloe out the café door. "I've had such a lovely time with you this morning and I'd like to continue spending time with you. Would you like to come back to my apartment with me?" Rudy asked boldly.

Perhaps it was the way he spoke fluent German that reminded her of Max. She obliged and they shared a romantic weekend at his apartment, making love and eating chocolate.

Rudy was the most charming man she'd ever met. He was full

of compliments and funny stories. He was sweeping her off her feet.

On Monday morning Chloe awoke to find Rudy sitting at the table in the kitchen. It was very early, but he was already dressed and ready to leave.

There was something about his demeanor that had shifted. He seemed distant.

"Are you going to work?" she asked nervously. He had never shared what he did for a living or anything about his life in Germany. Their attraction to each other had been immediate and physical.

"I'm going home," he said. "I was here on business, but now I'm heading back to Germany. I have a wife and children who are waiting for my return."

Chloe felt the room start to spin. "You're married?" she managed to choke out.

He nodded, his eyes hard like glass, before he turned and looked away from her.

How could I have been so stupid? Chloe thought. She took a deep breath. I can't let him see me cry.

"Well, you had better be going then," she said coldly.

Rudy's face softened for a moment. "I'm sorry. I know it's no consolation, but I never meant to hurt you." He stepped towards her and touched her face. She recoiled, feeling her cheeks grow hot with shame.

"It's just that you are so pretty and I couldn't resist. I haven't done this too many times before, but when I did it always ended amicably. The women and I have become friends." He smiled. "You see, although my marriage is unsatisfying in so many ways and I no longer love my wife, I can't divorce her. We have too many financial ties. She knows how I feel, but she refuses to let go, even though we don't sleep in the same bed or even the same room anymore." He paused for a moment. "Ah, well, sometimes things just work out that way, but I adore my children so at least something good has come out of this marriage. I'm afraid that I won't be returning to France any time in the near future, so this is goodbye."

Chloe sighed. He was the first man in her life that she had been wildly sexually attracted to.

"I'm sorry if I hurt you," Rudy said, sensing her sadness. "I should have told you at the start that I was married. I know that having weekends like this with strangers isn't good for the welfare of my children. Or for the women involved, like you. I hope you can forgive me."

But the more he talked, the angrier Chloe became. "You certainly weren't thinking about the welfare of your children when you climbed into bed with me. You're a cad, that's for sure. I just wish you were at least honest with me from the start." She glared at him.

"Please forgive me, Chloe. I was wrong to seduce you."

"What's done is done," she said firmly. "You might as well leave now. Go home."

"I can see that you're hurt, I'm sorry. Would it make you feel better if I tried to come to Paris to see you once in a while? I won't be coming this way for at least six months. But after that I could try to visit."

Chloe let out a hollow laugh. "No, I would rather you didn't."

"I understand. And... thank you for the wonderful weekend. The apartment is booked until this afternoon, so feel free to stay until then. I'll be on my way now." Rudy let out a long sigh. "Chloe, I want you to know that I'll never forget you," he said as he turned and walked out the front door. It closed softly behind him.

She shook her head and stood up. *What a vain and self-centered, good-for-nothing louse! I wish I'd never met him.* Chloe leaned against the wall and tears welled up in her eyes. *What do I want? I'm so confused,* she thought, as she lay down on the bed. *I felt like I could never have feelings for another man when my heart is still so attached to Max; I was sure that I would never make love again. But Rudy was so charming that he somehow made me believe that it might be possible that I could someday marry again. I'm so lonely. I need to feel close to another person the way I felt with Max. But I can't seem to fall for the right men. If Lily were here with Mimi, then I would not need a lover. My heart and my days would be full. But as it is, I miss them terribly. And I know that I must face facts, Max is gone. And Lily is living her life in America with her husband and her daughter. So, what's left for me?*

Chloe stood up and got dressed, grabbed her handbag, and looked in the mirror. *Every day I can see that I am getting older. My hair is not as luxurious as it once was, and my eyes have lost some of their youthful sparkle. I'm depressed and lonely. Sometimes it feels like it's not worth taking the time to cook for myself when I know I am going to be eating alone. And then this man came into my life and for this weekend I felt alive again. Like a beacon of light, Rudy entered my dark and lonely world. For a few moments in time I felt almost like life was going to begin again for me. However, now I see that it was all an illusion. I have only myself to rely on. So, that's what I will do. And this time, I mean it, I will never allow another man to touch my heart. I think it's best that I just go on alone and wait until the time when God sees fit to reunite me with my husband.* Chloe walked out of the beautiful apartment and made her way back home.

From that day on, Chloe refused every man who tried to invite her on a date. When she wasn't working, she spent her time pruning and caring for her garden or meeting dance students who needed extra help. And although she loved the ambitious young dancers, they could not fill her empty cup. Chloe found that she was unable to sleep through the night. Her thoughts were consumed with her daughter and her grandchild. Unable to return to sleep, she would lie in bed and talk to Max, wishing he was there beside her.

At least once each week Chloe wrote to Lily. Lily, in turn, wrote back. Although Chloe loved reading about Mimi's first day of school or receiving Mimi's drawings, this long-distance correspondence made her separation from them even more painful. All Chloe wished for was to see them again.

FIVE

1930

One morning, half an hour before her first dance class of the day was scheduled to begin, Chloe was busy getting ready for work. She had recently showered and was in her bedroom getting dressed when she thought she heard a knock at her apartment door.

She quickly slipped into her black ballet leotard and pink tights. Her hair was combed but still damp as she wrapped it into a bun on the top of her head. As she reached for her ballet slippers she heard another knock, louder this time. As Chloe rarely received visitors and no one ever stopped by this early in the morning, she was concerned. *Why would anyone be dropping by to see me so early in the morning? The only reason I can think that anyone might come is if there is a problem at the studio, with Maurice or one of the students. It might even be something worse—it could be news from America about Lily.* She quickly threw her housecoat over her ballet uniform and went to answer the door.

She opened the door to a well-dressed man and a pretty young woman. Standing behind them, hand in hand, were a serious young boy and a slender little blonde girl.

It couldn't be.

It was as if time had stood still. Chloe tried to catch her breath and steady her racing heart.

The little girl looked exactly like Mimi. *Could this be Mimi?* She peered at the child with golden blonde hair and bright blue eyes. A memory flooded her mind—clutching baby Mimi to her chest at the train station all those years ago. Taking in the sweet smell of her skin and praying that Joe would look after her beloved family and keep them safe.

But why would Mimi be in Paris without Lily and Joe? Who are these strangers? she thought desperately. "Can I help you?" Chloe asked weakly, dread beginning to coil inside her stomach.

SIX

As Nick, his mother, and Friedrich walked out the front door, Chloe caught a glimpse of Friedrich looking at the *mezuzah* on the door frame. She could have sworn she saw him visibly flinch, but perhaps her eyes deceived her. Nick glanced back. His eyes were wet with tears, but he tried to give Mimi a reassuring smile.

Then the door closed behind Friedrich, Gloria, and Nick. They were gone.

Chloe could barely breathe after hearing about her daughter's death at the same time as being reunited with her beloved granddaughter. Her precious Lily was gone but here was Mimi.

Mimi sat timidly, her small hands folded in her lap as she kept her eyes fixed on the floor.

I'm a stranger to her, Chloe thought as she crouched down and gently took little Mimi's hand in hers. "Mimi, I know you don't remember me... you were just a tiny baby the last time I saw you. I'm going to take care of you, and I promise to never let anything bad happen ever again."

Mimi was alone with the person who she knew was her *bubbie*, but even so this woman was unfamiliar. Mimi tried desperately to recall some of the stories her mother told her about her *bubbie*, but her mind was cloudy. Even though every time her mother had mentioned her grandmother who lived in France, she had wanted to meet her, she realized now that she didn't know her at all.

For a few moments Mimi sat silently with her eyes fixed on the floor and her small hands folded in her lap.

"Mimi," Chloe said gently, but Mimi's shoulders began to shake. She longed to pull the child into her arms and hug her tightly, so tightly that the pain would go away for them both, but Chloe was afraid she might scare Mimi. She decided that it was best to allow Mimi to come to her in her own time. *Even if it takes a year, I'll wait*, she thought, filled with love for her granddaughter. *This poor child has suffered such trials and lost so much. And she's so young—how can she ever comprehend everything that's happened?*

Chloe waited. It would not have surprised her if Mimi began to scream or cry, or even if the little girl asked her why she had been left with an unfamiliar woman in a foreign country. But when Chloe looked into Mimi's deep blue eyes, she could see that Mimi understood far more than any child her age should understand. It was as if Mimi knew that Chloe was suffering, too.

Mimi moved slowly towards Chloe and laid her head on her lap. Chloe gingerly touched Mimi's soft blonde curls. Her small head was warm and sweaty. Chloe leaned down and kissed Mimi's forehead. Then to Chloe's surprise, Mimi whispered in a soft voice, "Gloria said you are my *bubbie*. My mother said so, too. She had a picture of you on her nightstand. That means you're my family. I know my mother loved you. So, I love you, too."

Chloe could almost feel her heart break.

"Yes, I'm your *bubbie*. And I love you more than you could possibly know," Chloe replied, gently stroking Mimi's curls.

"Nick said the word *bubbie* means grandmother in a strange language. Is that true?" Mimi asked as she looked up at Chloe.

"Yes, a *bubbie* is a grandmother, but the language isn't strange at all. It's Yiddish. Many people believe it's the language of God."

"If you speak the language of God, please can you ask him if he will send my mother back to us?"

Oh, this poor child, Chloe thought. "I wish it were that easy, darling. I would beg for your mother to come back. But I can't change things. I'm so sorry."

"Why did God take my mother away from me? I miss her and I need her."

"I wish I had an answer for all of your questions. All I can say is that we don't always understand why God does the things he does. But we must learn to accept his will. He has plans for us that we don't always understand." Chloe ran her fingers through Mimi's hair.

"Now Nick and Gloria are gone, too, and I'm scared," Mimi sobbed.

"I know, darling, but I promise that I'm here for you and everything will be alright. You'll see, I'll do my very best to be like your fairy godmother," Chloe said, trying to sound cheerful. "Do you know the story of *Cendrillon*? Cinderella, rather." Chloe adapted her language, conscious that Mimi had grown up in America speaking mostly English and a little French. "And do you know who her fairy godmother was?"

Mimi shook her head. "No. I've never heard that story."

"Ah, well, then you're in for a treat. Would you like me to tell it to you?"

Mimi nodded, eagerly drying her eyes. "Yes, please."

In a soft voice Chloe began the story, "Once upon a time..."

SEVEN

The day after Mimi arrived, Chloe and Mimi went to the local thrift store and purchased a small bed for Mimi. While they were there, Chloe noticed that Mimi was mesmerized by a painting of a princess in a tower. She saw her little granddaughter's eyes light up and felt her own heart swell. When she got to the cashier's desk, she whispered, "I'll take the princess painting, too." Then they went and bought pink sheets and a pink blanket. When they arrived home, Chloe set up a small space for Mimi to call her own. She made Mimi's bed up with the new sheets and hung the painting next to the bed so Mimi could look at it while she fell asleep each night. Chloe had cobbled together what little money she had to try and make Mimi feel at home.

A few days later, Chloe and Mimi went to the local school and registered Mimi for classes. Chloe could tell that Mimi was nervous and timid, especially as she wasn't able to speak much French. Mimi resisted and begged to stay home with Chloe, but while Chloe knew this was a lot of change, she still insisted that Mimi start school the following week.

Chloe and Mimi gradually began to settle into a new routine.

There were times when Chloe had to admit it wasn't easy trying to raise a child at forty-eight years old. Sometimes she would work all day and then take the bus to pick Mimi up at school. By the time Chloe got home she would be exhausted while Mimi, who was excited to see her grandmother, would be bursting with energy. She wanted to tell her *bubbie* all about her day at school. Although Chloe would desperately want to lie down for an hour, she didn't. Instead, she listened to everything Mimi had to say. It had been a long time since Lily was a little girl and somehow Chloe had forgotten all the trials and tribulations of raising a child. But because Chloe loved her granddaughter, she never lost patience with her. After dinner each evening, Chloe would help Mimi with her homework. After Mimi had bathed, Chloe would place her into the small bed and tuck her pink sheets around her. As Mimi looked at the painting of the princess in the tower, Chloe would tell her stories of maidens in towers being rescued by princes, or sing her the same lullaby she had sung for Lily. "Raisins and almonds, this will be your calling..." she would begin as Mimi drifted off. As soon as Chloe lay down, she would fall asleep. Chloe was genuinely tired, but happy; she no longer needed any sleeping medication to help her rest.

When Maurice asked Chloe if she would teach a dance class on the weekends, she agreed. Chloe brought Mimi with her, telling her granddaughter to stay at the back of the class and play with the doll that Chloe had made for her. But within two weeks Mimi was up and involved in learning ballet. She joined in with the rest of the class and even though the other students were older than Mimi —most were preteens and some were teenagers—they all liked her. Chloe marveled at her granddaughter's natural talent for the ballet. Before long, due to the coaxing of some of the other dance students, Mimi began to show an interest in music and in singing.

Maurice adored Mimi. She was a beautiful, graceful child. He took her under his wing almost immediately and asked her to call him Uncle Maurice. He told Chloe that he had always wanted to be a father and Mimi had given him this opportunity. Many times, when Chloe was short on money, Maurice would insist on paying for shoes and clothes for Mimi.

For the most part, Mimi was an easy and undemanding child. But one Sunday night as they sat at the dinner table, she refused to eat. She was shuffling her potatoes around on her plate and tears slid slowly down her cheeks.

"What's wrong, my beautiful girl?" Chloe rushed to kneel at Mimi's side.

"I hate school. I don't want to go tomorrow. In fact, I don't want to go anymore. The kids are mean to me, and they make fun of me." Mimi sobbed and took a big breath as Chloe rubbed her back gently. "They speak in French and I can't understand what they are saying."

Although Mimi was learning French, she had not yet mastered it, which made it difficult to make friends. She was too shy to try and answer questions in class because she was afraid of being laughed at.

One afternoon, Mimi's teacher called Chloe at the dance studio and asked if she could come in for a meeting. Chloe told Maurice, who offered to cover her last class of the day.

"Of course. Don't worry about anything. You go and take care of our little Mimi," he said reassuringly.

"Thank you," she said as she grabbed her coat and scarf and rushed out to catch a bus to the school.

Mimi's teacher was in the classroom waiting when Chloe arrived.

"Mrs. Levin," the teacher addressed Chloe sternly.

"Yes."

"Mimi is your granddaughter. Am I correct?"

"Yes, ma'am."

"I'm afraid to tell you she is not doing well here. It seems Mimi is unable to pay attention during her classes. She is daydreaming while I am teaching. When I ask her a question, she is usually looking out of the window. This is very disruptive to the rest of the students. It must stop."

"Of course," Chloe replied though she felt anger rising within her. "But you must try to understand that Mimi's mother passed away recently. She's just a child and she's been through a great deal. She misses her mother terribly, just as I do. Besides that, until recently Mimi lived in America, so she doesn't speak fluent French. It must be difficult trying to listen to a teacher when you don't understand the language. I promise you that Mimi is a good girl and her French is improving every day."

"I understand all of this, but this daydreaming must stop. I have other students to think of. I cannot spend all day watching Mimi. I'm sure you understand."

Chloe clenched her fists by her side, but she couldn't risk losing Mimi's place at the school. "I'll speak to her tonight."

Over dinner that evening Chloe asked Mimi about everything she had discussed with Mimi's teacher. All that Mimi would say was, "I don't care if I never make any friends at school. The other children don't like me anyway. I wish Nick was here."

"Now, I'm sure that's not true about the other students not liking you. I know that all the girls in ballet class adore you."

"That's because they're older and they think I'm cute, but I'm not a doll, *Bubbie*. I'm a person with feelings and I feel very lonely most of the time. I miss Nick. Is he going to visit us soon?"

"I don't know," Chloe replied sadly. She couldn't lie to Mimi and Gloria hadn't been in contact.

"Can you write to him and ask him to come?"

"I don't have an address to write to."

Mimi's lower lip trembled as she stood up. Chloe pulled her into an embrace and kissed her forehead. "It's going to be okay, I promise," she whispered.

"Good night, *Bubbie*. I'm going to bed," Mimi replied sadly.

Chloe's heart broke as she watched her turn and walk into the bedroom.

Chloe wished she could have written to Gloria to ask her if Nick might spend a little time in France during the summer holiday when his school was closed. *I was so shaken up that I forgot to ask Gloria for a forwarding address,* she thought regretfully. *Maybe Nick has forgotten Mimi now, too? He was only nine years old when they last saw each other.*

Although the preteen girls in Chloe's ballet class adored Mimi and often made a fuss over her, Chloe knew that Mimi needed friends her own age. Chloe's problems with sleep returned and she often found herself staring at the ceiling in the middle of the night wondering how to help her granddaughter. Finally, she came up with a plan.

One winter morning Chloe took Mimi by bus to the school. She dropped her off at her classroom and then went to the principal's office to propose her plan. She offered her services as a volunteer ballet teacher. "If you'll allow me to, I'll teach female students who are in the same grade as my granddaughter."

"When would you teach these classes?"

"I'll conduct them after school, twice a week."

Impressed by Chloe's credentials and her offer to teach for free, the principal was immediately interested in this opportunity. "We would love to have you, Madame Levin. When can you start?"

The ballet classes began on the first of February. After Chloe finished working at Maurice's studio, she took the bus to Mimi's school. The classes were taken in one of the regular classrooms.

As soon as Chloe arrived, her students were required to move the desks out of the classroom and into the hallway for the ballet class and then to return them afterwards so the classroom would be ready for the morning. There was a great deal of excitement amongst the students. After all, learning from a talented ballerina like Chloe Levin for free was an amazing opportunity. By the end of March, Mimi had made many friends in her ballet class and come out of her shell at school, too. She was speaking French more fluently and her marks had improved.

The months turned into years, and Chloe and her granddaughter became inseparable. Every morning, they got dressed for school and work together; every evening, they prepared their meals together; and after dinner they read books to each other. Their bond grew unbreakable.

Although Chloe and Mimi were Jewish, many of the other students in Mimi's school were not. To show how much they cared for Chloe's students, Chloe and Mimi baked cookies for them that they brought to the school Christmas party each year. In the evenings, Mimi's new friends would often visit their apartment. Chloe didn't mind when Mimi and her friends practiced their ballet in Chloe's living room; she would smile secretly, delighted that her plan had worked. Mimi was developing friendships.

EIGHT

1936

Early one morning, three days before Mimi's twelfth birthday, Chloe was woken by Mimi shaking her.

"*Bubbie*, I'm dying," Mimi said in a hoarse voice.

Chloe's eyes shot open. "What? What happened? You had a bad dream?"

"No, *Bubbie*. It's not a dream. My stomach hurts. It hurts really bad. I feel sick, like throwing up. And... well... when I went to the bathroom, I saw blood on my underpants. *Bubbie*, I'm bleeding from my insides. I'll probably be dead in an hour or two."

"Oy, what was I thinking? I forgot to have this discussion with you," Chloe said more to herself than to Mimi. Tradition had it that Chloe was supposed to slap Mimi when she got her first menstrual period, but Chloe couldn't bear the thought of doing that. Mimi already looked terribly frightened, her eyes large and wide.

When Chloe took Mimi's small hands in hers, they were ice-cold. Chloe sat up in bed and hugged Mimi to her chest. For a moment she closed her eyes and remembered the first time Lily had menstruated. A smile came to her face. Lily had not been afraid because Chloe had prepared her, and she knew exactly what to expect. *How could I forget to talk to Mimi about this?* Chloe thought. *I suppose it's because I didn't realize that she was almost a young lady. I still see her as a child.*

"When I die will I be with Mommy again?" Mimi asked, sobbing.

"Yes, I suppose that you will. However, you aren't dying, my love. You're just fine and you'll be around for a long time. It's my fault that you're so frightened. I should have explained all of this to you sooner. Let's go to the bathroom and get you cleaned up. Then we can lie down in my bed and I'll tell you all about what it means to be a woman. I'm going to explain how we have babies and how our bodies work."

After they came back from the bathroom, Mimi cuddled up next to Chloe and listened while she explained how to take care of the blood each month so that she would not ruin her clothing. Chloe also told her about how babies were made. She couldn't help but smile at the mortified look on Mimi's face.

After their chat, Chloe and Mimi went into the kitchen where Chloe made a pot of tea and cut up some fresh bread and cheese which she placed on a platter with some apples and grapes.

"I'm a little sick to my stomach. I don't think I can eat," Mimi said.

"It's alright. Eat what you can and then go and lie down for a while," Chloe said as she kissed the top of Mimi's head.

NINE

When Gloria and Nick had first arrived in Europe, they—along with Friedrich—took a train from Germany to Paris where they planned to drop Mimi off at her grandmother's apartment.

On the train from Germany to Paris, Friedrich had professed his love to Gloria and promised her that he would always treat her son as if he were his own child. "I love you, Gloria. And I love Nick, too. I want you to spend the rest of your life with me. Will you be my wife?" he had asked.

"Friedrich, as you know, I care very deeply for you and I appreciate everything you've done for Nick and me," Gloria had replied, "but I won't lie to you—it's just not right. I can't tell you honestly that I'm in love with you."

Friedrich had looked at Gloria with such pain in his eyes that she had to reach out and touch his cheek.

"I want you to know that I like you a great deal. I think you're a wonderful man, but my heart has been broken so many times that I don't think I'm capable of love anymore."

"I know you are. Give me a chance and I'll show you. Our relationship will make you forget all the pain you've suffered in the past." He paused. "Marry me, Gloria. Let me adopt your son and together we will raise him with all the love he deserves. Say you will marry me... please."

Gloria took a moment. A million thoughts went through her mind, thoughts of the men from her past. Of Nick's father and Lily's husband, Joe, but the one thought that stuck with her was the financial security that Friedrich could offer her and Nick. Then she looked Friedrich in the eye, and she nodded. "I will."

Gloria and Friedrich were married in Paris the day after they dropped Mimi off at her grandmother's house.

Friedrich, true to his promise, immediately filled out papers that permitted him to officially adopt Nick and make the boy an heir to his family's fortune. This shocked Gloria. She had never expected him to share his wealth with a child that was not his. No man had ever treated her or her son so well. Friedrich had kept his promise, so Gloria began trusting him and she started to let her guard down.

Friedrich did not work much. He kept an eye on his clothing factory by going in once a week to see how things were running. However, he was an attentive husband and father when he wasn't busy with the National Socialist Party. Friedrich was almost forty years old when he returned to Germany from America and Gloria could see that he was desperately searching for a greater purpose.

TEN

1936

For the most part Gloria was happy. She was beginning to see how her life could be with Friedrich, but one thing troubled her. On the day that they had brought Mimi to live with her grandmother, she had seen something in Friedrich that had disturbed her. Several years had passed since Nick, Gloria, and Friedrich walked out of Chloe's apartment, leaving Mimi behind, but Friedrich still warned Gloria that he had seen a *mezuzah* on the doorframe of Chloe's apartment that day and he had forbidden her and Nick to visit Chloe and Mimi.

Both Chloe and Mimi were blonde-haired and blue-eyed. No one, least of all Friedrich, would ever have suspected that they were Jewish without being told. As Friedrich was a staunch supporter of the National Socialist Party, its leader Adolf Hitler and his ideas for Germany, his realization that Chloe and Mimi were Jewish did not sit well with him. One night a few weeks after they returned from Paris, when Nick was in bed and Friedrich and Gloria were enjoying tea and pastries, Friedrich put down his spoon after stirring his tea and said, "Well, at least that's over."

"What's over?" Gloria asked.

"We dropped the little girl off with her grandmother."

"Yes, I miss Mimi so much, but I know that her mother would have wanted this."

"Well, I'm glad we won't be living anywhere close to Mimi. We're going to be staying right here in Berlin and that's far enough away from Paris to keep Nick away from Mimi. Nick is still very young, he's just a boy." Friedrich sighed and lit a cigar. "If we don't talk about Mimi, he'll soon forget her. I'll keep him busy in the meantime. I'll make sure he knows that she's a Jew and that the Jews are responsible for all the evil in the world."

"You don't really believe that, do you?" Gloria asked, bewildered.

"Absolutely. I've seen it with my own eyes," he replied confidently.

"I haven't," Gloria said dismissively. "I had a wonderful relationship with Lily, and I knew she was Jewish. It never mattered to me. She was one of the kindest people I ever met."

"Well, Lily is gone and it's best for Nick to stay away from anyone who is Jewish. Things are changing here in Germany and the further he is from having any Jewish friends, the better."

Gloria fell silent, unable to articulate what she wanted to say.

"All the while Nick is growing up here in Germany, the country I love, I'll be a true father to him. We'll do all the things my father never had time to do with me. I'll teach him to speak German fluently and I'll instill pride in him and love for his country. We'll attend National Socialist Party meetings together and he'll come to love it as much as I do. Then, of course, Nick will start school here as well and then he'll make lots of friends his own age. In a year or even less, he won't remember Mimi."

Friedrich and Gloria's conversation about Nick being kept apart from Mimi had taken place six years ago, but neither Nick nor Gloria had ever forgotten Mimi.

During those six years Nick grew into a handsome young man. While he was impressionable, Friedrich took Nick with him everywhere he could. He took him to the factory where he taught him about the family business. Friedrich explained that Nick was the sole heir to his family fortune and that he should therefore learn everything he could about running the factories. Nick went to the parties and social gatherings hosted by Friedrich's friends and neighbors, and although Friedrich was hardly a hunter or a fisherman, he tried for Nick's sake to take him camping along with a group of several other fathers and sons of a similar age. Friedrich purchased the best equipment available for the camping trip. They went into the forest where they set up tents and went fishing and hunting for their food. But Nick didn't like it. He loved animals and he hated killing things. Friedrich didn't enjoy the outdoors much either. Over the four-day trip neither of them caught nor killed anything. Instead, they both ate the food the maid had packed for them before they left. They were famished when they returned home.

Although Nick was young, Friedrich found him to be an insightful and intelligent boy who seemed much older. Friedrich saw no reason to wait to get Nick involved with the National Socialist Party and he began to take Nick with him to meetings that mostly took place in taverns. Nick felt like a grown-up at the meetings, especially when Friedrich allowed him to drink an occasional beer.

ELEVEN

One lazy Sunday afternoon, Friedrich took Gloria for a walk around the grounds of the sprawling estate that his family owned. He showed her where his grandfather had carved a heart with his own name and his grandmother's name into a large oak tree.

"That's so romantic," Gloria said, blushing.

"There's so much of my family's history all over the estate," Friedrich replied. "Would you like to see the room where my father was born?"

"Yes, of course," Gloria said, smiling. "I want to learn as much about you and your family as possible."

They walked towards the back of the house. "This is the room where my grandfather and father were born," Friedrich said as he opened the bedroom door. "Can you believe that?"

"Were you born in Germany, too?"

"Yes, I was. But I don't remember much of Germany, because my parents left for America when I was only a year old. I don't have any childhood memories here, but I love my German ancestry, and I am very proud to be German." Friedrich smiled proudly. "I hope you are, too."

"Of course I am," Gloria said, although she had never given her German ancestry much thought until she had married Friedrich.

It took the whole morning to cover the grounds of the estate on foot, and it was almost one o'clock when they headed back to the house for lunch. As they arrived back at the house, Gloria called for Nick. "Go and wash your hands," she said as he walked into the living room. "We're going to have lunch now. You must be very hungry!"

"Yes, I am, Mother," he said and then he smiled at Friedrich.

Friedrich winked at Nick, and Nick winked back.

They had a maid and a cook, but Gloria didn't feel the need to summon the maid. She just went into the kitchen, quickly whipped up three cheese omelets, and cut three thick slices of bread from the loaf that she had baked the day before.

"You can always have the cook do this," Friedrich said to Gloria as they all sat down at the table. "Although I love your cooking—the cook would struggle to make meals as delicious as this! Don't you agree, son?" he said, smiling at Nick.

"Yes," Nick said.

"However, I wish you would allow the housekeeper to do the rest of the work around here. You shouldn't have to worry about washing clothes or cleaning the house."

"It's not necessary. I don't mind taking care of the house," she said.

"Are you sure? I hate to see you work so hard."

"Of course, I am," Gloria said, smiling. "It gives me something to do. I want to be useful."

"You are useful. You make me happy," Friedrich said. "Did you enjoy walking around the estate and seeing the grounds?"

"It was lovely and very interesting. Your home is a beautiful place."

"There's still a whole area you haven't even seen yet," he said.

"Really?"

"Yes, the attic. It's where my family stores unused furniture. I've only been up there a few times myself, but I've heard it's haunted."

"Haunted?" Nick asked excitedly. "Really?"

"That's what everyone says," Friedrich answered and then took a bite of his bread.

"Can I come up with you both, so I can see it, too?" Nick asked.

"Sure, but I'm warning you, it's scary. It's dark and it's dusty up there." Friedrich knew he was playing right into Nick's fascination with adventure. "There are probably big hairy spiders and massive spiderwebs."

"Gee whiz! I want to go up there right after lunch," Nick said.

"You know better than to use slang terms like that, Nicholas," Gloria gently reprimanded him.

"I'm sorry," Nick said, "but please can we go up and see the haunted attic?"

"Only if your mother wants to go," Friedrich said.

"I don't mind." Gloria smiled. "I'd love to see some of the old furniture."

"Who knows, there might even be ghosts up there," Friedrich said. He smiled and winked at Nick.

Nick smiled back at Friedrich.

"But Nick isn't afraid. He's a superior man. He's a pure Aryan. Aren't you, son?" Friedrich said.

"Yes, sir," Nick replied, sitting up straight and proud.

Nick knew the term Aryan, and he understood the meaning of being a superior man. He had learnt it from the National Socialist Party meetings he had attended with Friedrich. The concept of being considered a superior man pleased him. So, like Friedrich, Nick was quite taken with, the Chancellor of Germany, Adolf Hitler. Nick had heard Hitler speak at a meeting once and was drawn in by his charisma. Nick loved the special and important feeling he got when Hitler spoke of the superiority of the Aryan race. As he enjoyed being a part of something, he didn't pay too much attention to Hitler's rants about his hatred for Jews. In Nick's mind, he did not associate Mimi with Jewish people, but he still thought about her. Sometimes Nick told his mother how much he missed Mimi, but she always avoided his questions when he asked her if she still had Mimi's grandmother's address.

Once they finished eating, Friedrich insisted that Gloria allow the housekeeper to clean up. He lit a candle and the three of them walked up a flight of stairs to a hatch which opened to the attic. Friedrich was right, it was dark and there was dust everywhere. Gloria sneezed several times in a row.

"Do you want to go back downstairs? I realize it's very dusty," Friedrich asked.

"No, really. I'm fine," she said.

They walked through the huge, eerie attic space guided only by the light of the candle flame. Two overstuffed chairs stood in the corner. They looked hardly used, and Gloria could tell that they had once been very expensive. Outdated dresses and suits that appeared to be brand new hung on a clothes rack; in another corner was a lumpy old mattress without sheets.

When Friedrich saw Gloria eye the mattress he said, "That was my grandmother's. I loved her dearly. In fact, she was the reason I fell in love with Germany. When I was a child and she was still alive, my parents would bring me here every summer to visit her. She was quite the lady. Very elegant and beautiful. She lived here with my uncle and his wife, and they had a cook and a maid. But when I came to visit, my grandmother refused to let the cook bake cookies for me—she did it herself. She always said that it was because I was her one true love." He smiled, reminiscing about his grandmother. "At the time I never thought about when she had shifted that sentiment from my grandfather to me, but he was already dead, so I don't suppose it mattered!" Friedrich laughed. "Oh yes, she went into the kitchen and baked cookies just for me. Sometimes I would get up very early in the morning, before my parents woke up, and I would dash into my grandmother's room and wake her. She didn't mind; she was never angry with me. Instead, she would take a book off the shelf in her room and read to me. I can still remember how I would lie on her bed and listen to her read. Those were wonderful times. So, when she passed away, I couldn't bear to get rid of her mattress, but by then it was so lumpy that it was too uncomfortable to sleep on. I couldn't put it in one of the bedrooms, so I moved it to the attic."

"I can understand how you felt," Gloria said. "The mattress was full of memories. I wouldn't have thrown it away either." She paused, spotting an old sewing machine on the other side of the attic. "Does that sewing machine work?" she asked Friedrich.

"I don't know. I mean, it should. But no one has used it in years."

"Can I try? Can we bring it downstairs so I can see if it works?"

"Sure. Of course. I'll have one of the servants bring it down this afternoon." Friedrich smiled. "I didn't know you could sew."

"I can. I can make clothes, and curtains. And... well, I suppose you could say I can make pretty much anything."

"You are a wonder, my dear. I'm so happy you came into my life, Gloria. I'm so proud of you. You're the perfect German *hausfrau*," Friedrich said.

"The chancellor would love you, Mother," Nick said proudly. "He thinks women should be good cooks, but frugal. He would be very impressed by your sewing skills, too."

Gloria smiled but her lips quivered. "He hates Jews, doesn't he?" she asked.

"I suppose you could say that," Friedrich said carefully. "I would say that he can see how damaging the Jews have been to the Fatherland. He thinks we should keep an eye on them. They are not to be trusted."

Just then there was a tap on the tiny window in the corner. They all turned at the same time to see a black crow staring through the window at them.

TWELVE

Nick had always longed to have a father. He saw other boys with their fathers and wondered what it might be like to have a male role model to teach him about life. He had always been careful not to hurt his mother's feelings. Now that he was older, he realized how hard it must have been for her to raise him on her own.

When they met Friedrich, everything changed. At first, he found that he resented this new man who took so much of his mother's attention, but the more he got to know Friedrich, the more he found that his stepfather was everything he had been hoping for as a child. Friedrich never treated Nick like a little boy. Friedrich made Nick feel more like a friend than a child. Delighted by Friedrich's interest in him, Nick began to emulate his stepfather.

They often had lively discussions about the state of the world, especially the state that Germany was in following the signing of the Treaty of Versailles. And because Nick had been too young to understand that Friedrich's hatred of Jews would also include Mimi, he was easily swept into the Nazi doctrine that his fellow National Socialist Party members constantly professed.

For Nick, the National Socialist Party meetings were gatherings of a group of friends. The boys he came to socialize with were the sons of party members.

He would play football on Sunday afternoons with the sons of the other members of his National Socialist group. There were many social gatherings and sometimes pretty girls who were the daughters of party members attended as well. Almost everyone that Nick associated with was a member of the party. Even though the Nazi doctrine that Nick was taught was often cruel and fanatical, he soon accepted it as the normal beliefs and opinions of the people he knew.

In the six years since Nick last saw Mimi, time raced by. He had been enjoying his friendships and having fun. He learned to speak German like a native, but he had always missed the little blue-eyed girl that he had spent some of his early childhood with. At first, he couldn't understand why his stepfather was so against him seeing Mimi. Friedrich would explain how the Jews were an evil blight on the world. Everyone in the National Socialist Party seemed to share the same belief. Nick nodded along when they shared their views, but deep down he was conflicted.

It was delightful to be living in a big house, and not as the nanny's son as he had in Lily and Joe's home in America, but as a member of a family. It also made Nick happy that Friedrich treated him like his own son.

At night before Nick drifted off to sleep, he would often smile to himself and think that he now had everything a boy could want. Each week, he received invitations to attend parties at the homes of his friends. He also regularly attended school dances where he wore custom-made suits designed by Friedrich's tailor. The girls who he met at these dances were not children of party members, so he was not expected to treat them respectfully. Many of his friends, who were the sons of party members, had sex with these girls, but they would only consider marrying the daughters of other party members.

At the age of fifteen, Nick happily lost his virginity in the back of the football stadium when he was seduced by a girl from his history class. She was a cute little redhead with a sassy disposition that made him laugh. However, after he brought her home to have dinner with his family, Friedrich warned him, "There are girls for sex, not for marrying. You are going to want a wife who comes from a good family. It would behoove you to only date young ladies whose fathers are party members. The higher their status in the party, the better. Do you understand me, son?"

"Yes, sir," Nick said, but he didn't understand. He liked the girl, and she liked him. She was sweet, funny, and kind, but her parents were older, and her father had no interest in politics.

And so, to keep his stepfather happy, Nick stopped seeing the cute little redhead. It didn't break his heart, but he felt bad when she cried as he broke off their relationship. After that, he was more careful about who he dated. He didn't like breaking hearts.

It broke my heart to say goodbye to Mimi, but I know this is how it must be, Nick thought. *Father keeps telling me that we come from different worlds. I will always remember Mimi, and she will always have a place in my heart, but that's where we must leave things.*

THIRTEEN

Friedrich was generous and he gave Gloria all the material things that she had struggled without in her earlier life. There was no longer a lack of food. Gloria never had to worry about her son going to bed hungry, and Nick had a bedroom of his own. In fact, Nick's room was larger than the entire apartment where Gloria and Nick had lived in America before Gloria first met Lily. Friedrich often had to travel to nearby countries for business and most of the time he took Gloria and Nick with him. Gloria loved to walk on the beach or to hike up into the mountains. One night, after he made passionate love to her, they discussed their most recent trip to Italy.

"I loved it so much—the food, the weather, the magnificent landscape," she said, smiling at the memory.

"I'm glad you like Italy," Friedrich said, running his fingers gently over her breast.

"I loved Spain and Greece, too. I never in my wildest dreams thought that I would see these magnificent places."

"They are quite lovely," he said. "And it seems to me that you enjoy warm weather."

"I do, especially after living through so many New York winters."

He smiled at her, his eyes glowing with affection.

Friedrich seemed to be the perfect husband. He did everything he could to fill Gloria and Nick's lives with joy. As time passed, Gloria realized that she had grown to truly love him.

"I love you so much, Friedrich. I don't know how I ever lived before I knew you," she said.

There was a long silence before he spoke. "I don't know what to say," he replied awkwardly.

"Just say you love me, too."

"Yes, of course I do," he said. This was enough for Gloria. She turned over and fell into a blissful sleep. How could she know that once she had admitted to Friedrich that she adored him and could not imagine her life without him, he would begin to grow tired of her?

FOURTEEN

Everything in Friedrich's life had come too easily to him. He had never worked hard or struggled. His family had plenty of money and all the comforts that came with it. For as long as he could remember, his family's garment factories had thrived. Friedrich had no understanding of poverty, labor, or scarcity. His needs and desires were so easily achieved that it was almost as though a genie in a bottle waited for his every command and fulfilled it as soon as he made a request. This included not only material things, but also extended to the women he met. Before Friedrich met Gloria, every woman that he dated had been more than willing to be his lover. And most, he knew, hoped for marriage with him. Yet, no matter who he dated, whether they were rich or poor, he could not imagine spending the rest of his life with them.

As Friedrich had never had to try to attract women before he met Gloria, he had been intrigued when Gloria said she didn't love him. When he first met Gloria standing on the dock in New York, waiting to board the ship that would take her and the children to Hamburg, he could instantly feel her distrust of him. Later he learned why. She told him that she had not had good experiences with men and because of this she did not give her heart easily.

Once he heard that he would have to win her heart, something inside of him immediately rose to the challenge. This had been his initial attraction to her. Friedrich was not dumb. He knew that because Gloria had come from poverty, she would eventually accept his marriage proposal. After all, he was very rich, and every woman he had ever met who was of marriageable age hoped to marry a wealthy man.

Gloria was honest with Friedrich. She told him that she would marry him, but that she was not in love with him. At the very beginning of their relationship, before she began to leach on to him, he was mad about her. They had the most stimulating sex he had ever had, and he believed it was because she refused to go to bed with him until they were married. Gloria was a good girl, and he liked that about her. Friedrich decided she was the kind of wholesome girl he had been searching for. When he made love to her on their wedding night, he immediately saw that she was not as sexually stimulated by him as he was by her. The other women who he had slept with had been sexually wild about him in bed. They did everything they could to make him want them, but it backfired on them. He didn't want them; he wanted to get as far away from them as he could. That was why he left New York and all its socialites and gold diggers to go to Europe in search of a German woman who would be a good *hausfrau*. Someone he might want to settle down with. Gloria had turned out to be that woman. At least that was how it was in the beginning.

After they were married, Friedrich learned that Gloria had many of the qualities he had been looking for. She was an excellent cook who didn't need a lot of money to prepare delicious food. He marveled at this. When he lived with his family in New York they had a cook who was pretty good, but she spent a lot of money on expensive cuts of meat. Gloria didn't need to buy the best ingredients to make her food taste good. She knew how to tenderize meat, and she carefully cut away the soft or moldy parts of fruits and vegetables instead of throwing them away. Not only could she prepare delicious traditional German dishes, but she also baked fresh breads and cakes which he thoroughly enjoyed. Friedrich had always been thin, but after a few months of eating the food that Gloria prepared he began to fill out and gain some much-needed weight.

FIFTEEN

After Gloria had curled up in Friedrich's arms and told him for the first time that she was in love with him, everything changed.

As they sat together eating their poached eggs the next morning, Gloria could feel Friedrich's coldness spread across the room like the chill in the air outside. She cleared her throat, desperate to change the atmosphere. "You know you've changed my life. Before you and I met, things were very difficult for Nick and me, but you've been a wonderful father to Nick and a wonderful husband. I want to thank you for being the extraordinary man that you are."

Friedrich gave her a tight smile before opening the newspaper that sat folded on the table beside him.

Over the next few months, Friedrich began to travel alone. He would make excuses for why Gloria and Nick couldn't join him when he went away on business trips. Then he began to stay out late at night at least three times a week, claiming he had to attend evening meetings.

Gloria could sense that there had been a change in him. Her fears were confirmed when one morning he told her that he planned to move out of their bedroom and into one of the guest bedrooms. Friedrich claimed that he needed to have his own room because there were times when he woke up in the middle of the night with ideas to improve his factory or his clothing line. He said that when this happened, he wanted to be able to jump out of bed and write down his ideas. He claimed that he was moving into his own room so he wouldn't disturb her. She tried to protest by telling him that she didn't care if he woke her up; his presence in her bed meant more to her than her rest.

"I'm running the factory here in Berlin and it's a very consuming job. I'm sure you realize that," Friedrich said coldly. "This is what I need in order to do my job effectively."

"Yes, I realize you have a very important job," Gloria said, but she knew that his decision to sleep in another bedroom had nothing to do with his work.

Gloria couldn't understand what had happened. Friedrich had been so in love with her; in the early stages of their relationship, it had almost felt like he was obsessed with her. In the past he had wanted to make love as often as possible, but now whenever she came close to him and tried to seduce him, he said he wasn't feeling well or that he was too tired.

Gloria didn't know what to do. She couldn't figure out what she had done wrong. Every day she grew more depressed and resentful. She tried to talk to Friedrich about her feelings, but he refused to speak about the situation. He always seemed to be rushing to go somewhere: somewhere without her.

SIXTEEN

Friedrich had once been charmed by Gloria because she was so different from the women he had grown up with. Coming from a poor family, she had learned early in life how to be resourceful.

Gloria had a strong sense of integrity and honesty was important to her; she refused to take advantage of anyone. It was endearing to see the way she was always willing to lend a helping hand. Friedrich believed that she fit the mold of the perfect Aryan wife that he was looking for.

However, now that the initial challenge of winning Gloria's love had worn off, Friedrich began to see her differently. One night they were invited to a party at the home of a wealthy family who had been friends of Friedrich's family. The couple hosting the gala had known Friedrich all his life. He had been friendly with the husband since they were both small boys; they had spent time together as children when Friedrich came to Germany each year to visit his grandparents.

The friendship had never really been a close one, but because they were both in the same social circles it had lasted through the years. When Friedrich and Gloria arrived at the party, he noticed how the women stared at her as she entered wearing a simple, inexpensive cotton dress, even though she could afford expensive tailored dresses. At the beginning of their relationship, he found it charming that Gloria was not materialistic like the other women, but for the first time he realized that she stood out in this crowd— and not in a good way. These women were like sniffing dogs and they could easily detect Gloria's lack of class and breeding. Previously Friedrich would have thumbed his nose at them because he was so smitten with her, but now as he watched her sitting alone at the table, not knowing what to say when she was introduced to his friends, he found that he was ashamed of having chosen her as his wife.

Friedrich tried to be as considerate as possible, but he could not bear to sit quietly beside Gloria the way that he had done in the past. He was bored and so he offered to get them both a drink at the bar. She agreed and he was relieved to get up and walk away from her.

That was when Agnes, an old friend of Friedrich's who had always been in love with him, caught his eye. She was wearing a tight-fitting black silk dress that exposed just enough cleavage to be enticing. Her hair shone like liquid gold in the twinkling light from the overhead chandelier. Diamonds sparkled at her throat and her wrists.

Agnes looks wonderful, he thought. *I don't remember her being so pretty, but she certainly looks stunning tonight.* "Agnes, it's good to see you again," he said as he walked over to where she stood looking calmly at the people on the dance floor.

"My goodness, if it isn't Friedrich Wagner. How are you these days, Freddy?" she asked with a glint in her eyes.

"I'm fine. Just fine."

"I heard you got married?"

"Yes."

"Is that the lucky girl over there?" Agnes said, indicating Gloria.

"Yes, that's my wife, Gloria," Friedrich replied. He could see the disapproval in Agnes' eyes and wished he could crawl under the floor.

"Oh yes, the girl from the ship," she said sarcastically before adding, "She's a pretty little thing, isn't she?"

He knew she wasn't being sincere, so he just smiled. "And you? What have you been up to?"

"Traveling. You know, the usual." Agnes replied with a light laugh. "Are you still involved with the National Workers Party? Someone told me that you had joined."

"Yes, I did. And you?"

"I'm very good friends with some women who are married to the men closest to our chancellor. So, you could say I'm all for the new regime. If they allowed women to join the party, I would."

"You surprise me, Agnes. I never knew that you had any political interests at all."

"Of course, I do. I love our Fatherland, and I can't wait to see our country returned to its rightful place of greatness in the world." She arched an eyebrow. "Let me guess, you aren't used to women having political affiliations. I'll wager that your wife isn't interested."

"Quite right," he said, "she isn't."

Their conversation continued and Agnes, having gone to charm school, now flattered Friedrich while subtly reminding him of his wife's shortcomings. He did not return to where Gloria sat waiting. He could feel her eyes burning a hole in his back, but he chose to ignore her. Instead, he spent the entire evening chatting with Agnes. He waltzed with her and every so often he would notice Gloria looking on, trying not to show how hurt and concerned she was that her husband seemed to be interested in another woman. However, he didn't care.

When the evening ended, he bid Agnes farewell.

"I'm so glad we had this evening together," she said as she slipped a piece of paper with her phone number into Friedrich's hand. He took the paper gladly and offered her his warmest smile.

"Well, I suppose I should go and collect my wife," he said.

"I hope to hear from you soon," Agnes replied, winking at him.

"Of course, I'll be in contact."

In the automobile on the way home, Gloria asked Friedrich why he had never returned from the bar with the drink he had promised her.

"Who is the woman you spent the entire evening with?" she asked sadly.

"She's just an old friend," he replied more sharply than he intended. "You really need to start being more independent. I can't sit beside you like a babysitter all night."

He could sense Gloria was hurt and they fell into a miserable silence. When they got home, she put on her sexiest lingerie and then began to rub Friedrich's back. She was doing her best to entice him to make love to her. In the past he would not have been able to resist.

"I'm not in the mood for this tonight. I'm tired. I'm going to my bedroom," he said coldly.

Gloria wept into her pillow.

The following day Friedrich got up early. He showered, dabbed on some expensive cologne and dressed in one of his finest suits. Then he went into the living room where Gloria was having a cup of tea.

"You look very nice this morning," she said. "Shall I have the cook prepare you some breakfast?"

"No, I must leave. I've got to go into town to check on the factory. I'll be home late."

"Alright," she replied, her voice breaking. "Will you be home for dinner?"

"I don't know. Go ahead and eat without me. I might be very late," he said as he walked out the door.

As soon as Friedrich left the house, he went to a public phone and telephoned Agnes. He asked her to meet him and she agreed. They met at a small restaurant where they were both certain they would not be recognized by any of their friends. By early afternoon they were laying naked side by side in her bed.

SEVENTEEN

The first three months of Agnes and Friedrich's relationship were filled with passion and excitement. They would meet in quaint hotels off the beaten path or take weekend trips to the south of France where Friedrich was sure he wouldn't run into anyone who would tell Gloria of his indiscretions. But four months into their affair, Agnes started to feel that the excitement was waning, and it was becoming a chore to find a place where they wouldn't be spotted.

As they lay in bed after a long session of lovemaking, Agnes curled into Friedrich, laying her head on his chest and gently running her nails across his chest. "All this sneaking around is getting exhausting," she said, sighing. "It would be a lot easier if you just left Gloria and married me."

Agnes immediately felt Friedrich's body tense up and his demeanor change.

"Well, Agnes," he said sharply, "I best be going."

He stood up and her head fell to the mattress. She watched in shock as he quickly dressed, buckled his belt, turned to her, and kissed her on the forehead.

"I'll call you," he said coolly as he left the room.

Agnes slumped in the empty bed in disbelief, grasping the

sheets around her for an hour before she could muster up the strength to get dressed and head to her home. As she pulled on her stockings she thought, *He has never been so cold with me, never. Our goodbye kisses are usually filled with passion and longing until we can see each other again. This was different. Why did I say anything? Why does Gloria have such a hold on him? She is nothing compared to me.*

Agnes waited for two weeks to hear from Friedrich, but he never called. She finally called him at the factory, but his secretary told her that Friedrich was not taking any phone calls unless they were from his wife. Agnes slammed down the phone onto the receiver. "His wife," she repeated, mocking the secretary. Her blood began to boil.

No one treats me like I'm dirt. How dare he! Does he really think his wife is the perfect German hausfrau? Well, I vow to find something on her that will repulse him so deeply that he'll have to come running back to me.

With nothing to do but obsess about Friedrich, Agnes formed a plan. If she was going to rid herself of Gloria, she needed to find some dirt on her. So, in her desperation to hurt Friedrich, Agnes began to follow Gloria.

EIGHTEEN

Gloria couldn't understand what she had done wrong. She couldn't figure out why her husband no longer brought her flowers or little gifts. She couldn't understand why he no longer desired her in bed.

When Friedrich went home to America because his mother was ill, Gloria insisted that he take her with him. At first, he refused, but she was so persistent that he finally gave in. Gloria was hopeful that the trip would give them time for him to rekindle his passion for her. She was desperate to regain what she had lost, but he was cold towards her. It was as if an invisible door to his affection had slammed shut, leaving her standing outside alone. She spent most of the voyage by herself in the cabin while he went on deck and socialized. On one occasion Gloria followed Friedrich to the dining room, but she retreated to their stateroom when she saw him dancing with another woman.

Gloria considered asking Friedrich for a divorce, but he was still such a devoted father to Nick that she was afraid her son would be angry with her. If she was going to leave Friedrich, she had to be sure Nick could accept it. Gloria decided that she had to make Nick see Friedrich for the cad that he was, so she decided to fulfil one of Nick's greatest wishes. Friedrich had made it clear to Gloria several times that he didn't want her or Nick to associate with anyone who was Jewish. When she asked why, he didn't explain, just replied with: "It's not a good idea."

Friedrich's behavior made Gloria become angry and vindictive. His eyes were cold when he looked at her and she could see that he was no longer in love with her. Gloria's affection turned to hatred. More than anything, she wanted to hurt him as much as he was hurting her. As she knew that Friedrich adored Nick as though her son was his own child, she decided that when she got back to Germany, she would take Nick to Paris to visit Mimi.

Nick had not gone with his parents to America because he couldn't take the time off school. As Gloria hardly ever saw her husband while they stayed with his family in America, she was alone throughout most of the trip. So, on a whim, she took a bus to the pawn shop where she had pawned Lily's brooch six years ago. She hardly expected it to still be there. However, when she walked in and looked through the glass cases, it was nestled on a display cushion. The pawnbroker had explained that it had been bought from him and then resold to him several times over the past six years. Gloria smiled. The brooch was expensive, but she had pilfered plenty of money out of the pants pocket of her husband's suit that morning before she left. She took the money out of her handbag and paid the pawnbroker, then she wrapped the brooch in an embroidered handkerchief, tucked it into her bra, and left the store.

This brooch is meant to go back to its original owner. That's why the people who bought it were forced to sell it back, Gloria thought as she boarded the bus to Friedrich's family's home.

A few days after they returned to Germany, Gloria decided to approach Nick about Mimi. It had been at least a year since Nick had mentioned Mimi to his mother and Gloria wasn't sure if he would still want to go and see her.

"So, my darling," she said tentatively, "I was thinking that you might like to go and see Mimi again. I know you loved Paris. We can spend a couple of days eating some rich French food and we can make a stop at your friend's grandmother's home. How does that sound?"

"Really, Mama? It sounds very good. I miss Mimi so much. It's been such a long time since I last saw her," Nick said, his voice filled with enthusiasm.

"Wonderful, but let's keep this visit a secret from your father until we return," Gloria replied. "If you tell him our plans, he might try to stop us from going. When we get back you can tell him that we went to Paris and that you saw Mimi."

"Why, Mother? We've never kept secrets from Father before."

"I can't answer that right now. You are going to have to trust me. Will you?"

"Of course," he said. "I always trust you."

"This will be fun. Let's go next week," Gloria said.

The next week they traveled from Berlin to Paris by train. After six years Nick finally saw Mimi again.

NINETEEN
PARIS, 1936

One crisp morning when the sun shone so brightly that it was almost blinding, Chloe stood looking out of the window as she prepared breakfast for herself and Mimi. She had woken up early and there was over an hour before they had to leave for work and school. Over the last few months Mimi had started taking the public bus to school by herself each day. At first, Chloe had been worried about Mimi riding a bus alone. Sometimes Chloe had to remind herself that, years ago, when Lily was growing up, her instinct had been to try and wrap her daughter up in cotton wool, but Max had encouraged Chloe to stand back and let Lily do things for herself. Chloe had found it hard. Now she had to let go of her protective instincts again and allow Mimi her independence, too.

A sudden "pang, pang, pang" on the tin roof signaled that it had started to rain, but unlike the gray, blustery storms they sometimes experienced, this was a sun shower. Rain was not unusual in Paris, but this morning a large rainbow swept across the sky; it seemed as if God had taken his paintbrush and illuminated the heavens in magnificent color.

Spring is such a beautiful season, Chloe thought. *No matter how difficult the winter has been, the earth still rejuvenates herself.*

Tiny sprouts of grass peeked their heads out of the ground, and buds had begun to form on the trees and bushes. Chloe hurried to finish preparing breakfast, then called Mimi to see the rainbow before it dissipated.

"Come, Mimi, breakfast is ready."

Mimi bounced into the kitchen wearing her school uniform, which was a green and blue plaid skirt with a white blouse. Her blonde hair was pulled back away from her face into a loose ponytail. *She looks so grown up*, Chloe thought.

"Before you sit down, I want to show you something," Chloe said, putting her arm around Mimi's shoulder and leading her over to the window. "Look at that rainbow," she said, pointing to the sky.

"It's beautiful, *Bubbie*," Mimi said as she stood looking out of the window in awe.

Suddenly there was a knock on the door.

Mimi turned to Chloe. "I wonder who that could be. It's so early and we aren't expecting anyone, are we?" Mimi asked.

"No, we aren't," Chloe replied as she went to answer the door. She almost stumbled back in shock when she saw the woman and young man standing outside.

"Gloria! And... Nick, is that you? My, you've grown!"

"Hello, Chloe, it's lovely to see you again. Is Mimi here?" Nick asked boldly.

"Of course," Chloe said. "Please, come in. Won't you both sit down?"

Mimi must have overheard Nick's voice because she came rushing into the living room, her face a mix of delight and surprise. Her eyes filled with tears. She ran into Nick's arms as soon as she saw him.

"What took you so long to come and visit?" she said breathlessly. "I would have written to you, but I didn't have an address. Your mom forgot to leave one."

"I'm sorry, Mimi. I did forget," Gloria explained. "I didn't realize it until Nick mentioned that we hadn't heard from you."

Mimi looked like she didn't quite believe her, and Chloe wasn't sure either. There was an awkward silence before Gloria said, "It looks like you're both going somewhere. I hope we aren't interrupting anything."

"We were just leaving. Mimi is off to school, and I must get to work," Chloe said. She sensed that there was a reason why Gloria had tried to keep Nick away from Mimi, but she had no idea what it might be.

Mimi suddenly looked sad, realizing her time with Nick would be fleeting.

Registering her granddaughter's disappointment, Chloe turned to Gloria and said, "But we can be a little late. It's been so long since Mimi and Nick last saw each other. Why don't you come into the kitchen? We can have a cup of coffee and chat while these two catch up."

"Are you sure? We could come another time. I don't want you both to be late," Gloria said.

"I'm sure. It's alright if we're late just this once. Seeing Nick again means a lot to Mimi."

"Yes, it means a lot to Nick, too," Gloria said as she followed Chloe into the kitchen.

Chloe put a pot of water on the stove to boil before she sat down beside Gloria.

"I'm sorry that it's taken you so long to come and see us again," said Chloe. "Has something made visiting difficult?"

Gloria didn't answer the question. "I'm also sorry that it's taken us so long. How has Mimi been? Have you had problems with her adjusting?"

"No, not really. There were a few things we had to work on in the very beginning, but now we're doing fine."

"I didn't want Nick to come back here to see Mimi. I was afraid a visit from him might remind her of all the painful things she went through," Gloria said, avoiding Chloe's gaze. "My husband Friedrich insisted that it would be best if Nick stayed away from her. So, I'm afraid that I kept him away."

Stay away from Mimi? But why? Chloe wondered. She looked

carefully at the woman sitting beside her. Gloria looked anxious and tired. Something was not right. "I can understand. But then why did you bring him here today? What changed?"

"Honestly, Nick has not stopped talking about Mimi since we left her with you. It's been over six years since we came to Paris, but he still mentions her every day. I finally gave in."

Chloe nodded.

"I have something for you," Gloria said nervously.

"Oh?"

"Last month my husband and I went to America. When we were there, I went to the pawn shop where I had sold a brooch that belonged to your daughter. I had to sell it to get the money to pay for passage to bring Mimi to you in France. However, I've always felt guilty about selling it because I know that Lily would have wanted you to have it. She told me that the last thing you said to her was that you were giving her this brooch to hold for you until you both met again."

"Yes, I remember that day." Chloe's voice cracked.

"Anyway, I was hoping to find the brooch when I went to the pawn shop, but I doubted that it would still be there after all these years. And yet, to my delight, there it was. I purchased it immediately and brought it to Paris today to give to you." Gloria took the old familiar piece of jewelry out of her handbag and passed it to Chloe.

Chloe's eyes filled with tears, and her hands trembled. She closed her eyes, remembering vividly how she'd placed the brooch in her daughter's hand and whispered, "Keep this for me, until we meet again."

"This means a lot to me," Chloe said. "You can't know how much."

"Lily came into my life at a time when things were very hard for me and Nick. She helped us so much," Gloria replied, her eyes brimming with tears. "She was such a good person, and I will never forget her."

Chloe stood up and threw her arms around Gloria's neck. In a voice cracking with emotion, she whispered, "Thank you."

Mimi sat down nervously on the sofa beside Nick. She stole a quick glance at him, noticing the fine hairs growing on his face and the sharp line of his jaw. He was no longer a little boy. She felt her cheeks reddening and she quickly looked down at her feet.

In a soft voice, almost a whisper, he said, "My mother wouldn't give me your address, and I was afraid I would never see you again."

"I was sure that you had forgotten me. I finally gave up begging my *bubbie* to find you. She said she tried but she couldn't. I know she was telling the truth because my *bubbie* never lies to me. Oh Nick, I've missed you terribly."

"Me too. I thought about you all the time," Nick said quietly before turning to Mimi. "Tell me what you've been doing with yourself. I mean, besides growing up," he added with a little laugh.

"You look even more grown up than me," Mimi said and then she frowned. "I mean, you're not old or anything. You're just... well... you're handsome."

"I knew what you meant," he said as he ruffled her hair just like he used to when they were little kids. "Want to take a stroll?"

"Sure," Mimi said. She called out to Chloe, "*Bubbie*, Nick and I are going out for a walk. We won't be long."

"Alright," Chloe called back. "I guess we'll take the day off from school and work," she said to Gloria, smiling.

As Mimi and Nick made their way down the street, they fell into a comfortable silence. From time to time, she noticed him watching her and she wished that she were prettier. She was at the awkward stage between adolescence and womanhood. She had begun to lose some of her "baby fat," as Chloe put it, but she still did not have much of a figure. When she looked in the mirror, Mimi saw a plain young girl struggling to grow into a woman. Her breasts were undeveloped, and she had no hips, although she was proud of the shapely legs she had developed due to her constant ballet practice. However, she never felt pretty. She was sure she was not one of the more attractive girls at school.

They walked for a while along the cobblestones, side by side. Nick had grown into a handsome teenager. At fifteen he was tall and no longer skinny. His body was trim, muscular and well-built. Mimi thought he was the best-looking boy she had ever seen.

"What are you going to do when you finish school?" she asked him. "Are you going to get a job? Will you stay in Berlin, or will you move back to America?"

He laughed. "You just asked me a whole bunch of questions all at once."

"I'm sorry." Mimi's face turned red as she looked away embarrassed.

"It's alright. I'm only teasing." Nick stopped her and took her hand in his. "You never have to feel uncomfortable when you're with me, Mimi."

She smiled shyly.

"As far as what I plan to do when I finish school, I'm going to work with my father for a while. A year or two. He says he needs me at the factory."

"That's right. I remember now, he owns a garment factory, doesn't he?"

"Yes, and he's getting older, so I want to help him as much as I can. He's been very good to me. However, in a couple of years I'd like to continue my studies. I'm hoping to get into the University of Munich. I would love to study literature and poetry. Someday I want to write a book."

"I'm sure you could do anything you want to do. I have faith in you."

"You always did," he said, smiling. "I can still remember when we were children and we were leaving New York. Do you remember that you whispered to me that you were so scared to get on the boat to Europe?" Nick paused to look at her. "You didn't tell my mother. I took your hand and promised you that everything would be alright and you believed me. You always turned to me instead of the adults. Do you remember that?"

"I do, I always felt safe when you were around," Mimi replied softly.

"I want you to always feel safe whether I'm here or not."

"Does that mean you won't be coming back to see me again?" she asked.

"I'll try to come back. I promise," Nick said.

"I hope you won't wait for a long time before you return," she said shyly.

"Well, I'm very busy with school, but I'll never forget about you."

"Perhaps you can even stay in France with my *bubbie* and me for a while."

"I'd like that," Nick said. "Paris is really exciting."

"I'd like that, too," she said. "Maybe we can write letters to each other until you're able to return? Will you give me your address?"

There was a short pause before Nick said, "Of course."

Mimi noticed something strange about his response; despite his obvious pleasure in seeing her, he didn't seem as enthusiastic about staying in contact as she was.

"You know," he said gently, "I didn't realize for some reason how much of an age difference there is between us. I mean, I always knew it, but I guess seeing you today, I realize..."

"I know I'm still a child, but I'm growing up fast."

"Yes, it's true, you are." Nick smiled.

"There's always been a special bond between us, don't you think?" Mimi asked Nick. "Do you remember that when we were children, we promised each other that someday we would get married?" She giggled.

"Yes," Nick replied in a serious voice, "but now that we're older, we both need to understand that what is between us is friendship."

"Please don't say that. I've always believed that someday you and I really would get married," she blurted out, feeling her cheeks grow hot.

"Married? How old are you now, Mimi?" Nick replied. He was startled by the strength of her affection for him.

"Twelve," Mimi muttered. *I'm so embarrassed. I want to die,* she thought.

He smiled. "Well, I'm afraid you have a long way to go before you're going to be thinking seriously about marriage."

She couldn't bear to look at him.

"Mimi, I'm sorry. I didn't mean to hurt your feelings."

"I wish you hadn't come here," she said as a single tear slipped down her cheek.

"Aww, come on, don't say that!"

"I mean it. I feel like you think I'm just a child and an ugly child at that." Mimi began to cry.

"Never, I didn't say anything of the sort," Nick said. "I don't think you're ugly."

"You think I'm a child."

"I think you're too young to be thinking about getting married."

"Well, I didn't mean that I think we're going to get married now. I meant someday."

Nick nodded. He reached out and took her hand. "I think you're very pretty and I'll always care about you."

"Really?"

"Of course, Mimi."

"Then will you do something for me?" she asked.

"If I can, of course I will," he said.

"Will you please kiss me? I want my first kiss to be from you," she said.

Nick bent down and kissed Mimi on the top of the head.

"Not on the top of my head, silly! On my lips."

Nick was a handsome boy. He had been invited to lots of parties and he had kissed plenty of girls at school dances, but kissing Mimi felt strange. She was only twelve. Still, he didn't want to disappoint her, so he quickly kissed her on the lips.

A broad smile came over Mimi's face as she looked away, blushing. "Do you really think I'm pretty?" she asked.

"Yep, I think you're still the prettiest girl I know."

Mimi giggled. "You can kiss me again if you want to."

"I don't think that's such a good idea. I think we had better head back to the house," he said.

It was early afternoon when Nick and Mimi returned to her home.

Chloe insisted that Nick and Gloria stay for lunch. While Chloe prepared a little bread, cheese, and salad, Nick and Mimi played a board game in the living room.

When lunch was ready, Nick and Mimi went into the kitchen and sat at the table across from one another. As they ate, there was a strange awkward silence that hung over the room.

Mimi knew that Nick and Gloria would leave soon and a wave of sadness washed over her.

Before he left, Nick took Mimi's hand in his and squeezed it. "I'm glad I came here to see you today."

"You think I'm too young for you, don't you?"

"Yes, I'm afraid that I do," Nick said. "Besides that, I think you're too young to be thinking about romance. If I were you, I would enjoy my childhood."

Mimi nodded and tried to stop the tears welling up in her eyes from falling.

"Listen to me, Mimi, you're very special to me and I don't want to hurt your feelings, but we live so far away from each other, and our ages are so far apart that I can't see anything romantic forming between us in the coming years."

"No matter what's happened in my life, I never forgot you, Nick," Mimi said. "Not for a single day."

"We're always going to be friends. Right?" Nick asked. He was sad to see his childhood friend so upset. "I don't want to lose our friendship. Let's write to each other once in a while."

Mimi could barely look at him. How long would it be before she got to see him again?

Later that night when Mimi and Chloe were alone, Mimi told her *bubbie* what happened with Nick earlier that day. "He thinks that because I'm only twelve, I'm just a child. He sees himself as a grown-up. But I'm not a child, *Bubbie*. I'm not. We're only three years apart in age. That is not so much. Maybe he thinks I've gotten ugly or something," she moaned.

"You could never be ugly, Mimi. You're a beautiful girl, both inside and out. I know this is hurtful for you, but at this point in your lives a three year age difference between you and Nick seems like a million years. You shouldn't worry about it. Enjoy your childhood. It goes by too fast."

"I'm afraid it won't go by fast enough for Nick and me to be together," Mimi said sadly. "He'll probably meet someone by the time I'm old enough for him to consider as a possible girlfriend."

Chloe could feel her heart breaking for Mimi. She turned towards her granddaughter, brushing a golden curl away from her eyes.

"If that should happen, then it wasn't *bashert*. That means it wasn't meant to be. And, if it isn't *bashert* for you and Nick to be together, then God has something even better in store for you. Whatever God has in store for you is what is best, whether it be Nick or someone else."

"Oh, *Bubbie*, I wish I could believe that."

"Believe it, my little one. *Bubbie* would never lie to you."

"Why do you think Nick and his mother came here, *Bubbie*? Do you think it was because Nick wanted to see me again or do you think it was something else? Maybe Gloria felt guilty about leaving me here without ever checking to see how I was doing?"

"Well, I'm sure Gloria thought about you often and Nick wanted to see you, too," Chloe said. "But Gloria came for another reason. She brought me something that means a great deal to me."

"Really? After all these years, I can't imagine what she could have brought. Can you tell me what it is?" Mimi asked.

"I can tell you. In fact, I was planning to tell you," Chloe said as she patted the sofa beside her to prompt Mimi to sit down. After she did so, Chloe said, "Before your mother left for America, I gave her a beautiful diamond pin that was very valuable to me. We were standing at the train station, and she had you in her arms. I will never forget how I felt as I looked at your tiny face. I was afraid I would never see you again."

"Oh, *Bubbie*, that's so sad."

"Yes, it was, but I didn't want to stop her. I knew how much your mother loved your father and so I let her go, but not before I pressed the pin into her hand. She didn't want to take it, but I needed her to have it, so I insisted." Chloe's eyes began to mist over; she took a breath before continuing. "I said the last words I would ever say to her. I said, 'Until we meet again.'"

"Oh, *Bubbie*. I don't know what to say."

"There is nothing to say, *mayn kind*, my child. She left and then she was gone. That's why this pin means so much more to me than just its financial value."

"Can I see the pin?" Mimi said. "I would love to look at it."

"Of course you can," Chloe said. She got up and walked into the bedroom. A few moments later she returned and placed the jeweled pin in Mimi's hand before sitting down.

The bright golden brooch shone in the overhead light and the stones sparkled as Mimi studied it, turning it over in her hands. "I remember this piece of jewelry," she whispered. "Sometimes my mother would let me look through her jewelry box. I always thought it was so beautiful. She wore the other pieces that she kept in the box, the ones my father gave her, but she never wore this one. I remember asking her why she didn't ever wear it. She brushed my hair out of my eyes and kissed my forehead, then she said that she never wore it because she didn't dare lose it. She said that as long as she had it in her possession the day would come when she and I would see you again."

Chloe pulled Mimi towards her as they sobbed in each other's arms. Lily might have been cruelly taken from them, but they still had each other.

TWENTY

After Nick's meeting with Mimi, he and his mother went back to their hotel room.

"How was your visit?" Gloria asked her son.

"I don't know what I was expecting, but I somehow didn't realize that Mimi would still be a little girl. She's only twelve and I'm a man."

"You're only fifteen. Soon the three year age difference between you won't matter at all," Gloria said.

"I'll always care for Mimi, but, well, our age difference matters to me a great deal right now," Nick replied. "However, I promised to write to her."

"And will you?" Gloria asked.

"I don't know. I think perhaps it's best for her if I don't."

"Nick, I realize that Mimi is only twelve and she's still a child now, but in five years she will be seventeen and you will be twenty. The age difference won't be so apparent then."

He nodded. Then he said, "Mother, can I confide in you?"

"Of course, my darling."

"I thought she would be prettier. She was so pretty when she was little. Or at least that's how I remember her. Mimi is so skinny and awkward now. I guess I was expecting more."

Gloria laughed. "In five years, you won't be saying that. She's just a child on the brink of womanhood right now, but I'll bet she's gorgeous by the time she reaches seventeen."

He shrugged. "Maybe. But I might be involved with someone else by then."

"You might be, but my love, there is no rush," Gloria said.

TWENTY-ONE

Agnes followed Gloria and Nick all the way to Paris. As they entered Chloe's home, she stood in the shadows watching them. Having plenty of money and nothing else to do with her time, Agnes took a week and rented a room in the city so she could lurk outside Chloe's apartment and wait to see if Gloria returned. When she didn't, Agnes knocked on the door and pretended to be looking for someone else who lived in the area. A young girl who Agnes guessed to be around twelve years old answered the door. She was wearing a ballet uniform.

"Does Monsieur Picard live here?" Agnes asked innocently.

"No, I'm sorry, there's no one here by that name, you have the wrong apartment," the girl replied politely.

"I've traveled a long way, and I don't know where to find him," Agnes said. "Perhaps you can help me."

"I'm sorry, but I can't," Mimi said. "I wish I could help you, but I'm afraid I have to go. I'm going to be late for class."

"I see you're a ballerina," Agnes said, looking at Mimi's clothes.

"Oh, no. I just study ballet. My grandmother is the ballerina. She was famous when she was young. You may have heard of her, Chloe Mandel-Levin? She teaches ballet at a local studio now."

"Oh, yes. I've heard that name," Agnes said and then smiled.

"May I be so presumptuous as to ask... isn't that a Jewish surname?"

"Yes, it is." Mimi looked at Agnes suspiciously. "I really do have to go now," she insisted.

"Well, of course you do. How inconsiderate of me." Agnes forced a smile. "I'll be on my way."

Agnes knew that Friedrich was a staunch follower of the anti-Semitic Nazi regime. Now she had some ammunition against Gloria.

Agnes boarded a train back to Berlin that afternoon. As soon as she arrived home, she contacted Friedrich who tried to brush her off, but she insisted on seeing him. "I have some information for you that I think might be very useful."

"Oh, and what's that?" Friedrich asked. He was bored with Agnes but intrigued.

"I found out that your wife has a Jewish friend," Agnes said casually.

"What are you talking about? We have no Jewish friends," he said, clearly annoyed.

"You're quite mistaken about that. *You* may not have Jewish friends, but I can assure you that Gloria does." Agnes smiled before telling Friedrich what she had seen in Paris.

Friedrich was furious when he hung up the telephone. He had been sitting in his second-floor office and peacefully watching the workers on the factory floor before Agnes called. Now he was no longer feeling calm. "Get me a cup of coffee, Hazel," he shouted to his secretary. "Now."

Minutes later Hazel rushed in with his coffee. He was so angry with Gloria that he forgot to wait for his drink to cool down; he lifted the steaming liquid to his lips and took a large gulp. His body trembled with pain as he burned his lips, tongue, and the inside of his mouth. A curse directed at Hazel escaped his lips. As he placed the cup on his desk, his hand shook so badly that he knocked his drink over.

The hot coffee poured on to the pants of his suit. "Hazel," he called out, "you're fired!" He stood up and took his suit jacket off the hook where he had hung it by the side of his desk. Friedrich put his jacket on, hoping it would hide the wet spot on his pants, left the factory and headed home.

By the time Friedrich pulled up the winding path to his house he was fuming. The entire way home he had been consumed by anger towards his wife. His driver, who had been given the day off, met him at the garage. "I'll take the automobile from here, sir, if you'd like?"

Friedrich nodded, handing him the keys. His body still tingled with pain from the coffee burn as he stomped into the house and confronted Gloria. "Did you or did you not disobey me? You took Nick and went to Paris to see that Jewish woman. Mimi's grandmother. Didn't you?"

"Yes, I did. I'm sorry, Friedrich..." Gloria's voice trailed off.

"How could you when you knew how I felt about you talking to Jews? Yet, you went anyway and took Nick with you! Don't you care about his future, you stupid woman?"

"Yes, of course I care," Gloria said. "I'm sorry that this upsets you, but Nick has been wanting to see Mimi for a long time. I had something to bring to her grandmother, so we went. And that's that." Gloria paused for a moment, wondering how Friedrich knew about their trip to Paris. "Besides, how did you find out?" she asked.

"I know everything. You can't keep things from me, Gloria. Why would you ever want to? I've treated you and Nick very well and this is how you thank me! You bring shame to our family." Friedrich could feel his face flushing and he clenched his fists at his side. "It's bad enough that you would be so inconsiderate of my feelings, but you took Nick to the house of a Jew?" He shook his head.

"Yes."

"Can't you understand that you could ruin the boy's chances of rising to become a success in the Nazi Party?" Friedrich shook his head again. "You're turning out to be very stupid. I know you come from a dirt-poor, low-class family and you haven't had any education, but quite frankly, I never thought you would be so dumb."

"I'm sorry you feel that way," Gloria replied, but there was an edge in her tone even though she was visibly shaking. "Don't ever forget that Nick is my son. I am his mother, and I did what I felt was right as far as he is concerned."

How dare she! Friedrich felt his vision blur as he leapt towards Gloria and slapped her hard across the face.

The assault came so suddenly that she lost her footing and fell. Blood oozed from Gloria's nose as she lay sprawled on the floor. She stared up at him in disbelief.

Friedrich stood over her, his heart beating fast. "Make sure you don't take that boy anywhere near a Jew again or I'll make sure you're very sorry."

Later that evening Gloria locked herself in the bathroom. She finally worked up the nerve to look at her face in the mirror. The skin around her eye had started turning mottled shades of red and purple where Friedrich had slapped her. She began to cry; for the first time she felt that she had made a mistake in marrying Friedrich. She had never realized how cruel he could be, and she had never seen him turn violent before. Now she was afraid of him. Not only for herself, but also for her son. He was a powerful man with wealthy and influential friends. Gloria dared not try to leave him in case he decided to take revenge. But his behavior that day planted a seed of hatred in her heart that began to grow.

TWENTY-TWO

Mimi tried not to think about Nick. Her birthday was coming up and she knew her *bubbie* was planning a sleepover party for all the girls she had become friends with in her school dance class.

She wanted to feel excited, but she felt such a terrible sense of loss after Nick's visit that she was having a hard time being anything but sad. Still, she tried to put on her happiest smile when her *bubbie* was around and she hoped her *bubbie* would not see beyond it. Sometimes at night when she got ready for bed, Mimi would stand in front of a full-length mirror in her underwear and criticize her body. She was so skinny, with no breasts and no hips. Her lack of womanly gifts made her feel childish and unattractive.

As Mimi's birthday grew closer, her *bubbie* asked her what she wanted as a gift, and Mimi answered that she wanted a brassiere.

Chloe took Mimi to a woman's garment shop where she had Mimi fitted for her first brassiere. When Mimi put it on, Chloe could see that the tiny cup size made her feel even worse.

After they finished shopping, Chloe took Mimi out for a quick lunch. As they sat in a café a few streets north of the garment shop, Chloe looked over at Mimi's glum face while she picked at her food. "What is it, my love? You've been so sad lately and I don't know what to do to make you feel better."

Mimi shrugged. "I'm alright."

Chloe was not convinced. "Oh no, you're not. Please talk to me, Mimi, and I'll help you. I can't help if I don't know what's bothering you."

Mimi looked away, but she didn't say anything.

"From what I've gathered, this all started after Nick came to visit. Did something happen?" Chloe asked. "Did he hurt you in some way? Whatever it is, you can tell me."

"He doesn't like me anymore. He thinks I'm nothing but a child," Mimi blurted out. "He agreed to write to me, but he hasn't answered my letter, so I know he wants me to leave him alone."

"Oh, Mimi," Chloe said. She reached across the table to hold her granddaughter's hand.

"I'm ugly, *Bubbie*. I don't even look like a girl. Some of the girls in dance class have breasts already, but I don't. My figure looks like the body of a little boy. My hair is stringy and my face... Well... my nose is too big, and my eyes are too far apart."

"Mimi, Mimi, my sweet girl," Chloe said, gently squeezing Mimi's hand. "You're at an awkward age. I promise you that things will change. In a few years you will grow up. And when you do, your figure will fill out. You'll grow into your facial features, and you'll be beautiful."

"I don't know, *Bubbie*. I think I'm doomed to spend my life without ever finding a boyfriend. I always thought, somehow, that Nick would be that boy. But he isn't. I don't think I'll ever find anyone who is right for me. I think I'll spend my life alone as an old spinster."

"I don't think so," Chloe said. "Every girl goes through an awkward stage. It's just nature's way. You haven't grown up fully yet. In fact, right now, you are on the brink of becoming a woman. Give yourself a chance to grow up. You'll see that I'm right."

"What about Nick? I can't stop thinking about him and I don't think I'll ever see him again."

"I can't say whether you will or not, but I can tell you this: God has a plan for you and if Nick is part of that plan, he will be back. If he's not, then you will meet someone who will love you with all their heart."

"Really, *Bubbie*?"

"Yes, really. Put your trust in God, Mimi. He'll send you what you need."

TWENTY-THREE

BERLIN, GERMANY, 1938

Nick was waiting in the study for Friedrich when he returned home from work at the factory one afternoon. "Father, if you have a moment, I'd like to speak to you," Nick said boldly.

"Of course. What is it, son?" Friedrich replied as he sat down at his desk across from Nick.

"I want to join the army," Nick said firmly.

"Your mother will not be pleased to hear this. She was hoping you were going to attend the university in Munich."

"Yes, I know that. And I would like to do that someday, but not now." Nick paused. He took a deep breath and continued his well-rehearsed speech. "Father, our country is on the brink of rebuilding itself. Our chancellor is working hard to destroy that terrible treaty we were forced to sign at the end of the Great War, and I feel compelled to join in the efforts. I want to be a part of the future of our Fatherland. I want to help Germany become the world power it is destined to be. Our Führer is going to fulfil his promise to his people, and I want to be a part of that," Nick said with strength and conviction.

"Hmmm, I see."

"As the Nazi Party grows stronger, I want to grow with it. I would like to rise in the ranks and to make something of myself in the new Germany. Right now, I feel like attending university would be nothing but a waste of time for me."

"If this is what you want, son, then I'll help you, but let me speak to your mother. I think it will be better if it comes from me."

"Yes, sir. Thank you. Shall I stay home tonight?" Nick asked. "Perhaps after you speak with Mother, she will want to speak to me."

"Where were you going tonight?"

"I had plans to go out on a blind date. We're supposed to go to a *biergarten* to have a couple of beers and some pretzels."

"Sounds nice. Who's the lucky girl?" Friedrich asked. "You don't usually date much."

"I agreed to go on a double date with Gunther and his girl-friend, Charlotte. The two of them have become rather serious. Gunther says he plans to propose to Charlotte very soon. I suppose he's probably feeling sorry for me and so he's trying to help me find a girl. He thinks I want to get married as well, so he arranged this date. It was nice of him, but I'm not ready to marry. I want to join the army. I need to have an adventure before I settle down. Do you know what I mean, Father?"

"Yes, I know. Still, it's good for you to go out with girls. Just go out and have fun. When you're ready, the right one will come along. But for now, just enjoy yourself," Friedrich said.

"I don't think there is a right one for me. I find most girls rather immature and, well... silly."

"Women can be that way." Friedrich smiled. "But life is rather boring without them."

"I'm not really bored. I have you and Mother, and I have plenty of friends. What else does a fellow really need?" Nick said.

Friedrich laughed. "Well, I'm sure you have other needs, too."

"I find that when I become sexually involved with a young lady, she becomes too clingy and demanding of me," said Nick. "I suppose I might feel different if I met someone smart who is also from a good family. Someone I could not only share a bed with but also share good conversation."

Friedrich smiled. "Until you go out with this girl tonight, you won't know if she might be the one you've been searching for. What do you know about her?"

"Her name is Vera; she's a good friend of Charlotte's. They met at the secretarial school they are attending. But the truth is that I'm not too hopeful about the whole thing. I mean, look at Charlotte. She's not very attractive or terribly smart. I find her boring and a bit childish. How different from Charlotte do you think her friend is going to be?"

Fredrick laughed. "Point well made."

"I doubt they're going to be different at all," Nick said. "Quite frankly, I'm just going out tonight because Gunther is so insistent."

"You say this girl is going to secretarial school? What's her family background?" Friedrich asked.

"Her parents are factory workers. Rather unimpressive, I'm afraid," Nick admitted.

"And Gunther's fiancée? Does she have the same background?"

"Yes."

"And you say Gunther is planning to marry her? I know his father very well and he'll be livid," Friedrich said.

"Yes, probably so. Right now, from what I gather, both girls are nice, but they're from the lower classes. Not marriage material," Nick said.

"Hmmm, sounds like you can have your fun with this one, but don't get serious. When it's time for you to marry, you're going to want a girl from a good background. Someone who can help you rise in the party. Not just a good-looking girl. You understand me?"

Nick nodded. "But Mother was not from a good family, and you fell in love with her, didn't you?"

"Very much so. But that was before our chancellor made it important to have a wife with the right political influence. I want to see you make your way to the top. You're a handsome fellow and with my money and influence behind you, there's no telling where you can go. Where we can go together," Friedrich said. He smiled at Nick.

After Nick left the room, Friedrich sat back in his chair. Over the years he had grown very fond of his adopted son. He was proud of Nick's courage and his love for the Fatherland.

Friedrich knew that Gloria was going to be distraught at Nick's decision to join the army; he was sure she would blame him for it and threaten to divorce him. But he was also sure it would be an empty threat.

TWENTY-FOUR

Gunther, like Nick, had a wealthy German father who was well established in the Nazi Party. Both boys had access to automobiles. Gunther volunteered to drive to their date that evening. He arrived at eight o'clock, right on time, to pick Nick up. Charlotte and Vera were already in the car.

When Nick climbed in the back seat, Vera was waiting for him. She wore a white dress embroidered with red flowers. Her strawberry-blonde hair was curled perfectly. She had strong cheekbones, a prominent chin, and large, doe-like, soft blue eyes.

Nick studied Vera by the light of the moon; she wasn't bad looking. In fact, she was prettier than Charlotte. But, as he had assumed they would be, Vera and Charlotte were very much alike.

Vera was shy, so she spoke to Charlotte rather than directly to Nick. The girls giggled as they gossiped about the other girls at their weekly meetings of the *Deutscher Mädels*. As the evening wore on, Vera and Charlotte got into a serious discussion concerning things they learned from their *Deutscher Mädels* group. The importance of the German *hausfrau* had been stressed at every meeting. They knew all the responsibilities of running a German household.

As the girls talked, Gunther and Nick drank dark German beer and nibbled on pretzels with spicy mustard. Nick wanted to be interested in Vera, but he wasn't. He could not help watching the clock. He had hoped that he was going to enjoy his evening, but he wasn't having a good time; he was ready to go home.

Nick didn't express his desire to leave because he didn't want to spoil the evening for everyone else. Finally, Charlotte looked at her watch and said, "It's eleven thirty. Vera and I have to be back at our boarding house before we get locked out for the night. They officially close the doors at twelve thirty on weekends. If we leave now, we'll have an hour to talk in the car."

"Let's go then," Gunther said. "We'd better hurry."

Gunther insisted on paying the check and then the two couples left. Gunther drove quickly towards the boarding house, but just before they arrived, he pulled around the corner on to a deserted dead-end street and stopped. He turned off the car and Charlotte moved into his arms; she and Gunther began to kiss passionately.

Vera turned to Nick and smiled before leaning over and kissing him. She felt soft and pliable in his arms. His body responded.

After almost a full hour of steamy necking and petting, Charlotte looked at the clock. "We'd better hurry and get to the boarding house," she said breathlessly as she rebuttoned her blouse.

Gunther sighed and then he drove the girls to the front of the boarding house. It was twenty-five minutes after twelve.

"Just in time," a heavy-set housemother in front of the door said as the two girls ran up the front stairs escorted by Nick and Gunther. "Five minutes later and the two of you would have been sleeping out on the street for the night."

After the girls disappeared into the building, Nick got into the front seat beside Gunther and they headed off. As Gunther drove Nick home, he smiled slyly and asked, "So, what do you think of Vera? I mean, the two of you seemed to be getting along well in the back seat."

"She's very nice," Nick said.

"Yes, she is, isn't she? You looked like you were having a good time, so maybe we can do this again?"

Nick shook his head. "I don't think so. She's not for me."

"Why not? You don't have to marry her, but you can have a good time together. She really likes you. I can tell. She let you go pretty far tonight, didn't she?" Gunther asked.

Nick didn't answer.

"I'd wager that she would have let you go further with her if you'd tried."

"I'd rather not lead her on."

"You have too much integrity," Gunther teased Nick. "You'd have more fun in life if you didn't."

"Yes, I suppose you're right. However, in the past there were a few situations where I had sex with girls, and they promised that they understood that I didn't want anything serious. I believed them and for a while we had fun together, but then each one of them became possessive. They wanted more from me. And, quite frankly, I'm not ready to get married. Before I even consider marriage, I want to join the army. I want to do what I can to help our Führer rebuild our country."

"You've always been very concerned with the future of Germany and the importance of establishing the Nazi ideals," Gunther said.

"My father believes that Hitler has been sent from God to save our Fatherland. I think he might be right," Nick replied.

"Perhaps," Gunther said, adjusting his belt buckle. "But I'm not in the business of saving our country or anything else, for that matter. I would rather just enjoy myself. You know, a lot of people think Germany is going to go to war. Do you want to go to war? You do realize that you could die for the ideals you have in your mind. Do you really think it's worth it?"

"I would die if I had to in order to bring our Fatherland back to its rightful place in the world. Germany should be the pre-eminent world power. You and I both know that, Gunther. Besides, if you don't join and there's a war, you'll be conscripted anyway. I would rather join than be told that I must go. This way, I can show bravery and make a name for myself in the Nazi Party."

"Not me," Gunther said. "There is nothing worth dying for. My family is already looking for ways to keep me from being conscripted."

"If that's your choice, then you must do what you feel is right," Nick said, shaking his head. "But as far as I am concerned, I want to make my father and my country proud of me."

TWENTY-FIVE

BERLIN, NOVEMBER 7, 1938

On a chilly November afternoon, Nick sat proudly wearing his Nazi uniform inside a café with two male friends, who were also party members. They were sipping beer and discussing politics.

"Have you heard what happened?" Hans asked. He was a handsome young man—the proud son of a farmer; he had risen in the party due to his loyalty and good Aryan looks.

"I haven't heard anything," Alex, a less attractive but well-liked party member, said.

"A Jew shot a German diplomat in Paris," Hans spat in disgust as he jutted out his strong chin. "A Jew."

"Why?" Nick asked.

"What difference does it make? No Jew should ever attempt any act of violence against a German. It's appalling," Hans said as he slammed his fist on the table.

"I'd like to know exactly what happened," Nick said.

Hans took a cigarette out of his breast pocket and lit it. "Well, if you want, I'll tell you all the details that I know." He took a sip of beer and swallowed it. "This German diplomat, by the name of Ernst vom Rath, was living in France. Apparently, this Jew called Herschel Grynszpan was angry at the Fatherland because his parents were shipped off to Poland. So, he took it upon himself to get revenge by shooting vom Rath."

"That took some nerve. A Jew shooting a German official. Can you just imagine such a thing?" Alex replied. "Well, we mustn't let them get away with this. If they think they can do as they like, they'll try to take over our country."

"Yes, I have no doubt that they will. The Jews are a dangerous lot. They proved to be our downfall in the Great War," Hans said. "If it weren't for them, we definitely would have won."

Nick nodded, but he wasn't so sure that this was true. However, it was pointless to argue this fact with other devoted Nazis. "Did vom Rath die?" Nick asked.

"Not yet. He's currently in the hospital. But if he dies, I'm sure that there's going to be hell to pay for those lousy Jews. We'll make them sorry," Hans said.

TWENTY-SIX

NOVEMBER 9, 1938

It was a bitterly cold Tuesday evening as Nick and Friedrich walked into the large, well-heated *bierhalle* where they had been called to attend an emergency meeting of high-ranking local Nazi Party members.

"Do you want a beer?" Friedrich asked Nick after they had shed their coats, hats, and scarves. "I'm going to get one for myself."

"Yes, please," Nick said. He was surprised to see Joseph Goebbels sitting at a table at the front of the room, thumbing through a pile of papers. *Goebbels is an important man. I wonder why he has come here*, he thought.

Friedrich returned carrying two large beer mugs filled with dark liquid. He placed them on the table and sat down. "This meeting must be very important. It's by invitation only," Friedrich said.

"Yes, I knew that when we had to give the two men at the door our names before we were permitted to enter. I wonder what this is about," Nick said.

"I couldn't tell you, but I can see that it's top secret."

Nick nodded, taking a sip of his beer. He scanned the room. There were several men that he didn't recognize from their regular meetings. "I wonder what's going on."

One of the older members walked over to their table. "Friedrich, come with me, please. I need your help with something."

"I'll be back," Friedrich said to Nick.

Nick glanced around the room. The men were gathered into groups. He searched for someone he recognized so he could go and sit with them, but he didn't see anyone he felt comfortable joining. He continued sitting alone at the table waiting for his stepfather to return.

A few minutes later Joseph Goebbels stood up and raised his hands; the room went silent. "I regret to inform you that Ernst vom Rath died today. He was a German who was murdered for no reason at all by a Jew." He cleared his throat and paused for effect. "This sort of conduct by Jews must not be tolerated. We must make these filthy swine pay so that they know that the superior race is in power now and they must not dare to challenge us."

At that moment, Leopold, one of the young men who Nick had become friendly with from party meetings, walked over to Nick. "I'm so late," he whispered as he sat down beside him. "Has anything happened?"

"Not yet. Goebbels just started speaking," Nick whispered.

Leopold had also recently joined the army and tonight he looked exceptionally tailored in his new uniform. His blond hair was slicked back with cream to keep it in place, and he smelled of expensive cologne. Leo moved his chair closer to Nick so that he could speak to him without disturbing everyone else at the meeting. He whispered, "I hate sitting through these meetings. They're so long and often terribly boring."

Nick smiled politely at him, but he didn't usually find the meetings boring. Right now, he was trying to listen to what Goebbels was saying.

Leopold continued whispering, "I'd like to get out of here and meet some girls. Have you noticed that girls have been falling at your feet since you began wearing your uniform?"

"I'm sorry, I didn't hear you," Nick said sharply.

"Girls, I'm talking about girls."

"Oh yes, girls," Nick replied, but he wasn't listening to Leopold, he was attempting to hear what Goebbels had to say.

"Yes, girls." Leopold shook Nick's shoulder.

"What about girls?" Nick asked, annoyed by Leo's constant interruptions.

"The uniform. It's like a magnet for women. They love it so much that they just fall into bed with you."

Nick nodded. He had already found what Leopold was saying to be true. Women loved men in uniform. In Nick's experience, they were so impressed by his uniform that they offered themselves to him without him needing to make any moves at all. Recently, he had given in and stopped resisting easy, non-committal sex. In the past, he had been reluctant to sleep with women who he had no intention of ever seeing again. He was certain this was because when he was young, he had once overheard his mother crying. He had asked her why she was weeping, and she told him that she missed his father. Nick had asked, "Where did he go and why did he leave us?"

Gloria, hurt and upset, had responded honestly to her little boy: "I don't know, Nick. He left me because he never really loved me."

"Maybe it was my fault," Nick had replied. He still recalled how he felt that day. He had blamed himself, but his mother refused to allow him to take the blame.

"No, dear," Gloria had said gently as she brushed his hair out of his eyes with her fingers. "It's not your fault, I promise you that. It's just that some men are not good men. They lie and tell us that they love us and that they will be there for us, but then they abandon us. When you grow up, don't be this kind of man. Never treat girls like this. It hurts them."

On that day Nick had made a promise to himself that he would never lie to any girl. He would never say "I love you," if he didn't mean it.

"So, when this is over, do you want to go out and pick up some girls?" Leopold asked earnestly.

"I'm rather tired tonight. Perhaps some other time," Nick said wearily.

"Well, I'm going to try and find someone to go out with me after this is over. I'll see you at the next meeting," Leopold said as he left the table.

By the time Leopold left, the meeting was ending. A large group of young men had gathered at the front of the hall. Nick stood up and stretched his legs as Friedrich returned to the table. He stood beside Nick and said, "You're going with the rest of the young fellows, aren't you?"

"Where are they going?" Nick asked. He had missed most of Goebbels' speech thanks to Leopold, so he had no idea what was happening. Now he was secretly cursing Leopold for distracting him.

"What were you doing that stopped you hearing Joseph Goebbels giving you orders?" Friedrich asked.

"I'm ashamed to admit that Leopold was over here talking to me and I'm afraid I didn't hear the speech."

Friedrich shook his head. "Well, you need to join those other young men. You'll all head to the Jewish sector of town where you're going to make some mischief."

"Mischief?"

"Yes, you'll break a few shop windows. That sort of thing. We need to show the Jews who's boss here in Germany."

Nick felt a sense of dread creep into his stomach. It must have shown on his face because Friedrich gave him a stern look.

"What's bothering you about this?"

"There are women and children in Mitte," Nick replied quietly.

"Yes, so what?" Friedrich asked.

"Does this plan involve violence?"

"No, not violence. Just a bit of mischief. No one is going to get hurt. Now, hurry up and go over there and join the rest of the group. You really should go with them. It would look very bad for our family and for your future as a party member if you didn't."

"Yes, Father," Nick said. He didn't want to disappoint his father, but he had a bad feeling about this.

TWENTY-SEVEN

1938

The young men climbed into the back of an open-air truck. Goebbels' speech had filled them with excitement and the self-righteous anger that comes from a mob of unruly boys who have been told they have power and superiority. As the truck began to move, an icy wind slapped Nick across the face. He cursed softly under his breath, wishing he'd worn a scarf. *I never expected to be doing something like this on a cold night like tonight,* he thought as the truck raced towards the Mitte neighborhood where quiet, unsuspecting Jewish people were getting ready for bed.

No one else in the back of that open-air truck seemed to be bothered by the weather. They were feeding each other's bloodthirsty frenzy as they sang a song about hanging Jews. Some were yelling about how angry they were that a Jew had killed a German. Nick glanced at them in disgust. *I never knew vom Rath and I'll bet none of them did either,* he thought. *This is nothing more than an opportunity for them to run wild and cause trouble for the Jews. Well, I don't care what they doI'll break a window or two and then get back into the truck. Hopefully we won't be out too late. It's very cold tonight and frankly, I'm tired.*

But when they arrived at Mitte, Nick was shocked to see that the chaos had already begun. There were more groups from other parts of town who had arrived earlier, and the synagogue was already on fire. Orange flames leapt into the sky and smoke filled the air. Young men, some in uniform, many in regular clothes, could be seen dashing through the streets carrying burning torches. Screaming was heard as Jewish men and women tried to run away and hide from the mobs who were invading their neighborhood.

Nick had been getting out of the truck when he stopped and stood paralyzed for a moment, shocked by the sight in front of him. A few feet away, three teenage boys were beating an old man with a club. The man lay on the ground, moaning. Nick couldn't move. The truck driver shook him and said, "Come on, let's go. You can't just stand here, there are others behind you waiting to get out of this truck and on to the street."

The driver handed Nick a lit torch and he jumped down from the truck bed. As they got off the truck, each of the young men was handed a torch. Whooping and hollering, they took their burning sticks as they began to run frantically through the streets.

The sound of shattering glass unnerved Nick, and the smell of smoke was so strong that it made his eyes burn. A sudden explosion almost knocked him to the ground. He desperately wanted to leave Mitte and go home, but he couldn't, not yet. He had to make sure that the drivers saw him do something destructive before he went home—at least then he would not be a disappointment to his father.

As Nick walked slowly down the street, his eyes met those of a middle-aged Jewish man with a long dark beard and thick sideburns.

The man stared at Nick, desperate and pleading. "You're not like the rest of them. I can see it in your eyes."

Nick wanted to hit the man or do something that would prove he was just like the others, but he couldn't. Stunned by the horror of what he was witnessing, Nick stood frozen to the spot. He grabbed the man by the shoulders and whispered, "Hurry, get out of here and hide before you get hurt."

The man nodded; he quickly ran into a building close by and

disappeared. Nick extinguished the fire of his torch, but he still carried his stick so he could use it to break a window as soon as one of the drivers was available to witness it.

Broken glass crunched under Nick's boots as he made his way through Mitte. He turned a corner and that was when he saw her: a girl who looked like she was about thirteen years old. A young girl who looked just like Mimi. Three teenage boys stood over her; she was sitting on the ground begging the boys to leave her alone. They were laughing.

One of the boys tore the little girl's coat off and pulled her blouse open, and another boy lifted her skirt. She was weeping now. Nick wanted to vomit. For a moment he stood watching, unable to move, unable to leave.

"I'm first," one of the boys said as he undid his pants. Nick stared as the other boys held the girl down. She was kicking, fighting, screaming, begging, but they would not release her.

"Shut up," one of the boys said to her, "you're getting on my nerves." He slapped her hard across the face and a thin line of blood trickled from her nose.

Nick could no longer bear it. He ran over to the boys and with all his might he punched the boy on top of her directly across the face and yelled, "Stop it right now. Do you hear me? Stop it." Nick was consumed with rage. He began to hit the boys with the unlit torch. The girl scrambled to her feet. She pulled her skirt down and covered her breasts with her torn shirt. Grabbing her coat off the ground, she ran away as quickly as she could.

Nick stopped hitting the boys and stood there staring at them. "What were you doing? Have you gone mad?" he asked angrily. "You animals were raping a little girl."

"That hurt," one of the boys said as he rubbed his upper arm where Nick had hit him with the torch. "You have a mighty swing."

Nick figured that the boys did not turn on him because they saw his soldier's uniform.

"Look what you've done! She got away," one of the other teenagers moaned.

"Yes, I'm glad I was here to stop this maniacal behavior of yours. I'm sure your mothers would not approve."

"My mother hates Jews."

"Mine too."

"Well, what would she think if she knew you were raping a girl? Not only that, which is certainly bad enough, but the girl was just a child. What were you thinking?"

"Weren't you in our group? I'm pretty sure I recognize you. You were at the *bierhalle* with the rest of us. Didn't you hear what Goebbels said?" another of the boys asked.

"I heard," Nick said, despite realizing that Leopold's constant chatting had distracted him from Goebbels' speech.

"Why did you stop us then?" he asked.

"Because what is going on here tonight is not right," Nick replied. "Do you think that a man of a superior race would rape a child?"

"If Joseph Goebbels says it's alright, and he is the Minister of Propaganda, then it must be alright."

"You think that forcing yourself on a young girl is alright? You can't really believe that."

"Jews are not human beings," one of the teenagers replied. "They are subhumans so that makes it fine. It's not like we were raping a girl, we were just having fun with a subhuman. That's all."

Nick shook his head. "Don't let me catch you doing something like that again or you'll have me to contend with," he spat furiously before he stormed away.

TWENTY-EIGHT

On November 9 and 10, 1938, the winds of dark fortune began their descent upon the Jews of Europe. The Nazis unleashed gangs of thugs on Jewish neighborhoods. Jewish businesses were destroyed. Jewish people were beaten, arrested, and killed. Synagogues were burned. These fateful nights would come to be known as Kristallnacht, the Night of Broken Glass, and they would be the turning point that would begin to strip the Jews of all their human rights.

TWENTY-NINE

Nick got up early on the morning that he was expected to arrive at the train station to leave for his first army posting. Ever since the Night of Broken Glass, he had been secretly questioning the ways of the new chancellor and wondering if he had made a mistake by joining the military.

He had always hated violence, but until that night in Mitte when he saw gangs of thugs going wild with rage, he had believed that Hitler was taking the country in the right direction. Now he wasn't quite sure. However, he had already signed up and there was no chance of turning back now. He convinced himself that the night in Mitte was a one-off and would not be repeated.

Nick studied himself in the mirror. He had to admit that he liked the way he looked in his soldier's uniform. It made him feel strong, handsome, and powerful. A smile crept over his face as his mother entered the room. "I was hoping you would be awake before I had to leave for the train station," he said softly.

"Is your father going to drive you to the train?" Gloria asked.

"Yes, he's already awake and dressed," Nick said. "You know how he is. If he has to be somewhere at eight o'clock, he's ready to leave at six. He hates being late."

She smiled. "I know. He's always been that way."

Nick looked at his mother, who seemed tired and withdrawn. Her eyes were puffy with dark circles under them. He could tell that his parents were not as close as they once were.

"Do you like the uniform?" he asked his mother, smoothing down his jacket.

Gloria inhaled deeply. She walked over to her son and straightened his collar. "Oh, Nick, of course, you look very handsome in your uniform. I just can't help feeling that I wish you were going to university instead of the army."

"I know, Mother, but I feel very strongly about protecting our Fatherland. I want the important men in the party to know that I'm loyal and devoted to our Führer."

"I realize that. And I understand why you wanted to join the army, but I just wish you were on your way to study at a university rather than to be part of a militia," she said. Smiling a sad smile, Gloria added, "Studying is a lot less dangerous."

"Well, there's really no need for you to worry. I don't expect there will be a war anytime soon."

"I don't either, but I'd still prefer that you were going off to university. I suppose I've always wanted that for you," Gloria said. "Since your father can afford it, I hoped that someday you would graduate from university."

"I hope so, too, but not yet. Perhaps I'll go to university after I serve in the army. You know I've always wanted to do something that would make you proud of me."

"Nick, you're my son. I am always proud of you. I have always been proud of you." Gloria's eyes were shining with tears as she fixed his collar.

He swallowed the lump forming in his throat. "I'm glad. I wonder what it's going to be like to be in the army. Some of the other fellows in the Nazi Party say that it is a bit like a grown-up version of the Hitler Youth."

"I don't know about that. The Hitler Youth is a lot of sports, fun, and games. I believe that the army is much tougher. They train you to be a soldier in case there is a war."

"Yes, and I'm sure that they will train us rigorously," Nick said, "but it won't matter because there won't be a war. I'll just march around in my uniform looking very debonaire." He winked at his mother. "All the pretty girls will 'oooh' and 'ahhh' when they see me walk by." He laughed.

Gloria put her arms around Nick's neck and hugged him tightly. "I love you, and all I've ever really wanted was for you to be happy."

"I am happy, Mother. I am."

"I'll stop hounding you about the army if you'll just promise me something," she said, taking his hand in hers.

"What is it?" Nick asked. His mother's serious tone stopped him from laughing and joking.

"Once you've served your time in the military, I understand if you choose not to go to university, but I'd really love it if you would seriously look for a girl to settle down with. It would mean so much to me to have a grandchild."

He let out a laugh. "You want me to make a promise about this?"

"I really do, Nick," Gloria replied. "Will you at least consider it?"

"Of course, I will," he said reassuringly. He knew that she didn't believe him. He had dated plenty of girls, but he never seemed to want to get serious with anyone.

"Are you going to come with Father and me to the train station?" Nick asked.

"No, since I hate goodbyes and I know that I'm going to cry when you get on that train, I think it's better for me to say goodbye here." Gloria flung her arms around Nick and held him tightly. "You've always been such a good boy," she said, her voice cracking with emotion. "I will miss you every day, and I will worry about you terribly."

Nick shook his head. "Don't worry, Mother. Everything will be just fine. I'll write to you at least once a week."

"Do you promise? You have never broken a promise to me before," she said.

"I promise," Nick replied.

THIRTY

PARIS, DECEMBER 1938

"*Bubbie,* I read something very troubling in the newspaper," Mimi said as she sipped a cup of tea before leaving for school in the morning.

"Oh?" Chloe replied. She brushed away a stubborn curl that had fallen into Mimi's eyes.

At fifteen, Mimi was always finding things in the newspaper that she thought were of great importance, like the latest fashion trends to wear or which cosmetics to use.

Chloe poured herself a cup of coffee and sat down across from Mimi to listen. "What is it? What did you read?"

"I read that there was some sort of violent demonstration in Germany that involved the Jewish community."

"What do you mean?" Chloe was suddenly concerned. "What kind of a 'demonstration'?"

"That's what they're calling it, but it sounds like a pogrom," Mimi replied anxiously.

Chloe nodded, then she sighed and said, "The Jews in Germany have been having a very hard time, from what I hear. Maurice has a cousin who lives right outside Berlin. His cousin says that they are forced to register with the government and are made to wear a gold Star of David on their clothes to let everyone know they are Jewish. According to Maurice, lots of Jewish teachers have been fired from their jobs and Jewish students have been forbidden to attend schools that are not strictly Jewish schools or universities."

"That's terrible," Mimi sighed. "But from what it says here about this violent demonstration, things have gotten a lot worse recently. Look at this." She showed Chloe the article in the paper. "It says that last month gangs of German thugs ran through the streets of Jewish neighborhoods, burning synagogues and destroying Jewish businesses. Some Jewish people were hurt by these thugs as well. This is just awful, *Bubbie*."

Chloe shook her head. Mimi had not even been aware that she was Jewish until she came to live with Chloe. In fact, when Mimi had lived with her parents in America, she had celebrated Christmas every year with the families of the crime bosses her father worked for.

Since Mimi had arrived in Paris, her grandmother had helped her to see the beauty of being born a Jew. Every Friday night, Chloe had prepared a Shabbat dinner. They would pick up fresh *challah* bread from the Jewish bakery every Friday. When the Jewish holidays came around, Chloe explained their significance and they celebrated each one of them. To help Mimi feel a sense of community, Chloe also joined a synagogue. Sometimes at night before bed, she told Mimi biblical stories that made Mimi realize the price the Jews had paid to be called God's chosen people.

Chloe made sure that Mimi understood how much the Jews had suffered to keep their faith alive. All of this knowledge gave Mimi a sense of pride and love for her heritage.

"This article is just awful," Chloe said, looking down at the newspaper. "I feel terrible for those poor people who are being mistreated in Germany. I must admit, I'm glad we're here in France and not there."

"Yes, so am I," Mimi said. She closed her eyes for a moment and thought of Nick. *Nick is in Germany. How is all of this affecting him? His stepfather was involved with the National*

Socialist Party, wasn't he? That's the political party of Adolf Hitler, the chancellor who hates Jews. Could Nick possibly be an enemy to the Jews now? A boy as gentle and sweet as Nick... how could he ever be involved in something so heinous? It still hurts to think of him not answering my letter, but I suppose he realized that I was just too young, and he didn't want to lead me on. I should hate him, but I don't. I forgive him and I still miss him. Even now, after all this time.

"Mimi, *shayna maidel*," Chloe said as she wiped the tears from Mimi's cheek with her thumb. "*Oy vey*, you're very upset. You're crying. Please, my sweet girl, don't cry. I know you are kind and you have a big heart, but weeping isn't going to help those poor people in Germany." She rushed over and knelt next to Mimi, taking her into her arms. "There, there. Everything will be alright, you'll see. Don't you remember I told you that there has been hatred towards the Jews throughout history? Always. In every country. However, the Jews are God's chosen people, and it is by God's will that the Jewish people have survived. Don't worry about the Jews in Germany. I know that some Germans are acting irrationally now under this new leader of theirs, but don't forget that Germans are smart and they have a very civilized culture. I'm sure they'll put a stop to this soon."

"I hope so, *Bubbie*."

"I know so, sweetheart. Now, don't you trouble yourself anymore, alright?"

Mimi nodded.

"Guess what? I have a surprise for you," Chloe said as cheerfully as she could muster.

"You do?"

"Yes, I do." Chloe pulled a small, gift-wrapped box out of the pocket of her robe. "I was planning to give this to you this morning." She handed Mimi the box.

Mimi opened the box to find a tube of red lipstick. She let out a shriek of excitement. It had been at least a year since she had started begging Chloe to allow her to use cosmetics and up until now, Chloe had refused. Whenever Mimi asked, her *bubbie* always said Mimi was too young.

Mimi threw her arms around her *bubbie's* neck. "Thank you, *Bubbie*," she gushed.

"Do you like the color?"

"I love it," Mimi said with excitement oozing from her voice.

Chloe smiled. She could see that Mimi was momentarily distracted from her misery by her first tube of lipstick. "Can I wear it to school today?"

"I don't think the teachers will allow it, but aren't you and some of your girlfriends planning to go to a dance on Sunday night at the synagogue?"

"Yes, we are."

"Well, you can certainly wear it then."

"Oh, *Bubbie*, really?"

"Yes, but you should blot the lipstick, that way the color will be more natural. It won't be so bright. You don't want everyone to know you're wearing lipstick, do you?"

"Yes, of course I do." Mimi giggled. "I want all of the girls in dance class to know that I'm now grown up enough to wear lipstick."

Chloe couldn't help but laugh, too. She remembered being Mimi's age and how much she had wanted to look older and more sophisticated. Her mother had not allowed her to wear lipstick, so whenever she was doing a recital or going to a dance, she borrowed her best friend's lipstick, which she applied as soon as she was out of her mother's sight. "I know how exciting it is to look grown up. I remember feeling that way when I was your age. But red lipstick does look so much better if you blot it. Will you please try?"

"I will, I promise," Mimi said.

THIRTY-ONE

In 1939, Hitler rained bombs on his Polish neighbors. Within the following two weeks he overran the horrified people of Poland, stripping the country of her independence and forcing her under German rule. On May 10, 1940, Hitler turned his eyes towards France. By the end of June, France lay choking beneath the boot heel of the Nazi machine.

THIRTY-TWO

MAY 10, 1940

When the Nazis marched into France, Chloe felt as if a black cloud had descended upon her beloved country. She felt a terrible sense of impending doom. She had heard rumors about how much the Nazis hated Jews. The people who she knew from synagogue could be heard after services talking about the "Night of Broken Glass," or Kristallnacht, in Germany. They said that they had heard that the Jews in Germany were now forced to wear a star on their clothing to let people know that they were Jewish. There were boycotts against Jewish businesses, and marriages between Jews and gentiles were strictly forbidden by law. Everyone had heard about the bombings in Poland and how Hitler had broken his pact with the Polish people.

"These Nazis plan to take over all of Europe. Mark my words," Maurice had said only a week before the Nazis had taken France.

"What do you think they'll do to the Jews in Paris if they do take over?" Chloe had asked.

"Nothing more than they've done to the Jews in Germany. I wouldn't worry too much about it. It will be humiliating, yes. They will single us out, but in the end, it will be just like every other ruling class that has ever ruled any country. We Jews will continue to go on as before," he had assured her.

However, Chloe wasn't convinced. When she saw the Germans marching through town, the hair on the back of her neck stood up and a small voice, a tiny intuitive message, crept into her consciousness. A message that warned things were going to get very bad.

THIRTY-THREE

The Nazis invaded the north of France in May, starting by the borders of Belgium and Luxembourg. Paris technically remained an open city without any military force, to preserve its beauty, but the sinister cloud of the Nazis was moving in quickly.

Mimi could feel the dread settling in, but she had Chloe as well as lovely friends who all looked out for each other. They had become a tight-knit group after meeting through their local synagogue services. Her best friend was Rose, and Mimi thought Rose's name suited her very well because she was a petite girl with very dark brown hair and lips that looked like rosebuds.

The day after the singles' dance for young people was announced by the rabbi, Rose went to visit Mimi at her apartment. Chloe invited her to come in and have some tea. "I have some cookies, too, I just bought them at the bakery this morning. Would you like some?" Chloe asked.

"Yes, ma'am. That would be very nice," Rose said, smiling enthusiastically.

"Alright, have a seat and give me a minute to go and let Mimi know you're here. Then I'll make some tea and put out some cookies for you both."

Chloe left the room but returned a few moments later with

Mimi by her side. Then Chloe put a pot of water on the stove to boil for tea and began arranging cookies on a white china plate.

"Rose, how nice of you to drop by," Mimi said.

"Well, I actually came by to ask you something."

"What is it?"

"I'm planning to go to the dance at the synagogue next week. I hope Ezra—the rabbi's son—will ask me to dance," Rose announced proudly. "But I don't want to go alone. Will you go with me? I really hope you will."

"I don't know," Mimi said. She had so wanted to go but now she felt conflicted; since Nick's visit, she had shied away from boys. The truth was, Mimi never thought that Nick could possibly hurt her. But he had. Now she was reluctant to give another boy the opportunity to hurt her again. "I don't think I can, I'm sorry."

"Please. Please come with me, I don't want to go alone," Rose begged.

"I don't have a dress that's appropriate for a dance," Mimi said, looking for an excuse.

"You can borrow one of mine," Rose said.

"I'm so tall. Your dress will be too short for me." Mimi sighed. "Besides, I don't want to go."

"But it will be so much fun."

Chloe overheard the two girls talking as she placed the plate of cookies on the table between them. She turned to Mimi and said, "I'd love to buy you a dress to wear to the dance. We can make a day of it. All three of us. You, Rose, and me. What do you say?"

"I don't know, *Bubbie*. I'm not really interested in meeting any boys."

"That's alright, but you're such a good ballet dancer. I'll teach you how to dance in a ballroom with a partner. You'll have so much fun."

"Will you teach me, too?" Rose asked. "I know a little, but I'd like to be a better dancer."

"I would be more than happy to," Chloe said, winking at both girls. "Now, how does this sound? We'll have a private dance class, just me with you two girls. I'll teach you both to waltz. By the time we've finished, you'll be ready to dance the night away."

Both girls giggled and nodded. Chloe was happy that Mimi seemed to be excited and willing to attend the dance.

"Once you can dance, we three can make a day of it. We'll plan an afternoon when we can go into town, and we'll go dress shopping. How does this all sound to you?" Chloe asked.

"We can't afford a new dress for me, *Bubbie*," Mimi said. "Besides, I don't mind not going."

"Don't be silly. Of course you're going. As far as a dress is concerned, well, you'll be surprised what I can do." Chloe winked at Mimi. "I know dresses are expensive." She turned her attention to Rose. "But I happen to know of several resale stores where we can get a bargain. Once you both find something, I'll make a deal with the owner of the shop to make sure we get a good price."

"But it's hard to find something that's modern," Mimi said. "Most of the things at resale stores were donated by older wealthy women or sometimes by the families of women who died. The styles there are usually out of fashion."

"Ahh, but I can use a sewing machine and with a little stitch magic, I can change the style for you—one, two, three." Chloe snapped her fingers and both girls giggled.

"I have some money that my aunt gave me for my birthday, so I can use that to buy a dress," Rose said excitedly. She turned to Chloe and asked, "Please can you help me as well? I'll probably need to make my dress more fashionable, too."

"Of course I will," Chloe said.

"Oh, please let's do this, Mimi. Please? It will be so much fun!" Rose pleaded.

Mimi shrugged, then she nodded. "Alright. We'll do it."

Rose jumped up and hugged Mimi. Surprised by her hug, Mimi stepped back.

"I'm sorry. I didn't mean to squeeze you so hard. I'm just so excited," Rose squealed.

"You didn't. It's alright."

Chloe smiled. She was pleased that Mimi had friends and was going to attend this dance. It wasn't that she didn't like Nick, he seemed like a nice enough young fellow. However, he lived in another country, and he wasn't Jewish. Chloe had seen so many mixed marriages go sour because of the pressure that society put on them.

It wasn't that she believed Mimi was going to marry Nick— they were, after all, only childhood friends and Mimi was just about to turn sixteen. Mimi had her whole life in front of her, but Chloe knew her granddaughter the way only someone who loves another person can know them; she knew that Mimi still had very strong feelings for Nick.

She assumed that Mimi's strong attachment to Nick had grown due to the support and kindness he had shown her when she was a frightened child who had just lost her parents. Although it had been four years since Nick's visit, the bond that had been forged between him and Mimi when they were children still held Mimi's heart tightly in its grasp. It had been a very long time since she'd mentioned Nick's name, but Chloe could see that Mimi was still not over the hurt. She knew this because Mimi never attended any social activities where she might meet new boys. In fact, whenever a young man tried to flirt with Mimi when they went to the market, Mimi never flirted back. Sometimes she was even rude to boys to discourage their advances. This was why Chloe felt it was important that Mimi go to this dance with Rose.

THIRTY-FOUR

A couple of days later, after Chloe finished teaching her morning dance classes, she went home to pack a simple snack for the girls for their shopping trip. The previous day she had had fun teaching them to dance the waltz and the foxtrot. Mimi was already pretty good at it and Rose seemed a natural. As she cut up an apple and some bread and cheese, Chloe sighed.

Maurice is so kind and he pays me enough for Mimi and I to live comfortably, she reflected. *He always tries his best to take care of me, and he brings in lunch most days of the week. I hope I never have to ask him for a raise, but the older Mimi gets, the more she needs things. Raising a young girl on only my teaching salary is a financial challenge. Ah, if only I had the money to take the girls to a café, I would. I'm tired and it would be so lovely to have a nice hot coffee served to me. Mimi would really enjoy going out to eat, too, particularly with a friend. Well, it doesn't matter, because as much as I would do anything for Mimi, I can't afford to spend money unnecessarily right now. This is the best I can do, especially since I am going to have to pay for a dress for Mimi, and who knows how much that's going to cost?*

Chloe took a few bills out of the jar of money where she kept her savings and put them in her handbag. Then she finished packing the picnic basket and sat down on the sofa to wait for the girls to arrive.

It was only on rare occasions that Chloe and Mimi went out to eat in a restaurant. When they did, it was mostly for a special occasion, and it was usually Maurice who had invited them. He always paid the bill. Chloe leaned her head back on the sofa. The birds outside were chirping softly as a warm breeze danced through the living room window. Her eyes began to close and she drifted off to sleep. In her dream, Lily was the same age as she had been the last time Chloe saw her when they had said goodbye at the train station. Chloe's heart ached for her daughter as she hugged Lily close to her in the dream.

"I miss you, Mama," Lily said. "I missed you every day that I lived in New York. I never forgot the lullabies you sang to me or the way you held me when I was frightened. I always wanted to go home. I wanted to go home to Paris and to you."

"I've missed you, too," Chloe whispered. "I have never gotten over losing you. When I first learned of your death, I wanted to end my own life just so I could be with you. I know that might sound selfish, but I couldn't help it. If it hadn't been for Mimi, I would have."

"It's not selfish," Lily replied. "There have been many times that I wished you could come and join me here on the other side. I know the time will come when we will be reunited because no one is ever gone forever. Death is not final. I learned this after I died. We will be reunited at the right time: in God's time. I know that as much as I miss you, you can't come here right now. Mimi needs you."

"Yes, she does. She has grown up to be the most beautiful, kind, and loving young lady. All I can tell you is that I love her so much. She is my sunshine, the light and joy in my life," Chloe said.

"She loves you, too. I can see it. You see, I'm always watching the two of you. I'm always with you both."

Chloe suddenly felt someone shaking her; the vision of Lily began to fade as she jolted back into consciousness.

"*Bubbie, Bubbie*, are you alright?" Mimi was shaking her hard. Chloe's eyes opened and she saw the terror on Mimi's face.

"You were so pale, just lying there. Oh, *Bubbie*. I was scared."

"Ssh, ssh, it's alright, my love. I'm fine," she said gently. "I just fell asleep." Chloe smiled at Mimi. "Don't worry. Nothing is wrong." Chloe wrapped her arms around her precious granddaughter, longing for Lily to be with them now.

THIRTY-FIVE

"Alright, you two, go and freshen up, and then we'll get going," Chloe said, trying to hide the sadness in her voice. Mimi and Rose went into the bathroom and quickly washed their faces and freshened up their hair.

Chloe ducked into her bedroom and fixed her hair in the mirror. Her eyes began to water; she was overcome with emotion thinking of her daughter. *Oh, Lily, I miss you so. You would have loved to come with us today. Mimi is going to her first big dance and we're going dress shopping. I know you'll be there with us, but the joy it would bring you to see how beautiful she is going to look. Our little Mimi is growing up.* Chloe took a tissue and dabbed her eyes before going to wait for the girls in the living room.

"We're ready, *Bubbie,*" Mimi said as she and Rose walked into the living room, smiling.

"Me too, girls," Chloe said with a big smile.

"I brought all the money I earned from babysitting my neighbor's daughter last summer and all the money I got for my birthday," Rose said. "I had more, but I had to give some of it to my parents. If I'm very careful, I think I have enough to buy a dress."

"*Bubbie,* if we can't afford it, I won't go," Mimi said. "I don't care. It doesn't mean that much to me."

Before Chloe could answer, there was a knock at the door. She got up and looked through the peephole. "It's Maurice," she said, opening the door.

"Good afternoon to my favorite girls," Maurice said, smiling.

"Good afternoon," Mimi said with a grin. She adored him.

"So, a little bird told me that you're going to your first dance?" he said, a mischievous glint in his eye.

"Perhaps. I don't know yet," Mimi said. "Let me guess, was that little bird my grandmother?"

"Absolutely right," Maurice replied, flinging a cape around himself. "Don't be silly, of course you're going! Now, your *bubbie* told me that you were planning to go shopping today. Is that true?"

Mimi shrugged. "Yes, *Bubbie*, Rose, and I were just getting ready."

"Well, every girl should have a special dress for her first dance, and I insist on buying your first formal dress. So I'm here to tag along on this lovely shopping spree."

"We can't let you do that," Chloe said.

"I'm not asking whether you'll allow me to do it, I'm insisting on doing it," Maurice said. "Let's go into town and have a nice dinner, but first we'll hit the couture shops and find something absolutely perfect." He grinned, rubbing his hands together with delight.

Rose looked down at her handbag. She took out her change purse and began to count her money. "I thought we were going to the resale stores. I don't have enough money to go to a couture shop," she replied sadly.

"Please don't worry about it. I'll buy you a dress as well," Maurice said, smiling.

"Maurice, really?" Chloe asked. "It's going to be expensive."

"Why make money if you can't enjoy spending it with friends? Mimi is like a daughter to me. And since Rose is Mimi's friend, that makes her my friend, too. Chloe, I want to do this. Please allow me to."

Maurice was such a darling man. "Are you sure?" Chloe asked.

"Very sure. I want to go into town to Levitan's department store to buy some furniture for the studio. So, my dear ladies, let's go shopping. After all, it is my favorite pastime."

"Oh, Maurice." Mimi threw her arms around his neck. "You are so wonderful."

THIRTY-SIX

They went to every couture shop on the Champs-Élysées and tried on every dress in their respective sizes. Chloe was exhausted and getting hungry, but she couldn't help but feel joyous at seeing how much fun Mimi was having. She and Rose were laughing in the carefree way that Chloe thought young girls should be able to. For a moment, Chloe paused and watched them. It made her smile that even in these uncertain times with the Nazis lurking around every corner, love and laughter still filled these young girls' hearts. It made her think of Lily, and she knew that her daughter would have loved to be there with them. Thoughts of Lily made her eyes sting with unshed tears, but she wouldn't cry. She wouldn't do anything to ruin this day for Mimi.

Finally, with Maurice's help, Rose picked a lilac-colored dress and Mimi settled on a satin gown of Wedgwood blue that brought out the color of her eyes. Maurice had the seamstress fit each dress to the girls perfectly and then they caught a taxi to Levitan's department store. It was an elegant furniture shop located on Magenta. As Maurice selected a new sofa for the waiting area in the studio, the two girls walked through the displays of well-made, stylish bedroom sets.

Mimi and Rose wandered the aisles of the department store

with awe in their eyes. Each display was put together with care. A living room had been furnished with a large couch and cushions perfectly placed to accent the vibrant colors in the drapery; it was illuminated by tall floor lamps and it contained a beautiful wooden coffee table with a travel book resting on top.

As the girls kept walking, they came across a dining room set for twelve people and they imagined what it would be like to have dinner parties or a large family to fill each set. They turned the corner and found themselves in the bed area.

"When I meet my husband and we get married, we're going to buy this one," Rose gushed as she pointed to a very expensive white oak four-poster bed.

"They are all so beautiful," Mimi said. "This entire store is full of wonderful things."

"What do you want to buy when you get married?"

Mimi shrugged. "I don't know. I've never thought about it."

"Look at that one," Rose said.

Mimi gasped. It was a heavy bed with a canopy made of hand-carved wood. "That's gorgeous."

"Alright, girls. Maurice is finished here. Are you two ready to go for dinner?" Chloe asked.

"Yes," both girls chimed.

As they waited outside while Maurice tried to flag a cab farther down the street, they saw a girl walking with her mother. The girl was Mimi and Rose's age.

"Look, it's Monique," Mimi said as she rushed over to the girl. "How are you? I haven't seen you at the studio in a long time. Have you stopped dancing?"

"No, not exactly," Monique said. "My mother made me quit going to the studio."

Monique's mother gave her a dirty look. "Let's go," she said.

"Wait. Why did you quit? I mean, if it's cost-related, I'm sure my *bubbie* and Maurice can help," Mimi said.

The girl's mother glared at Mimi. "We don't want your help. We don't want help from Jews. Now get out of our way."

"I don't understand," Mimi said, feeling her cheeks grow hot.

"My mother and I have decided that I'm not going to a school owned by a homosexual Jew," Monique said abruptly. "That's all there is to it. Now, get out of our way."

Monique pushed past Mimi who turned to look at Rose. Rose was shocked. Her mouth hung open.

"Don't mention this to Maurice," Mimi whispered. "It would really hurt his feelings."

"I won't," Rose promised.

Maurice finally hailed a cab and the four of them went to dinner at a lovely café where they sat outside. There was a warm breeze, the food was delicious, and Maurice was charming. He told jokes that made the girls laugh, but even as she was laughing Mimi could not get her conversation with Monique out of her mind.

A week later, Rose was brimming with excitement when she arrived at Mimi's apartment on the night of the dance. Her beautifully proportioned, petite frame and perfectly arranged dark hair made her look like a doll. Chloe greeted her at the door. "Don't you look lovely," she said, smiling.

Rose beamed. "Thank you."

"Mimi is almost ready. Please sit down and I'll let her know you're here," Chloe said.

"Yes, ma'am," Rose said.

Chloe knocked on the door to Mimi's room.

"*Bubbie?*"

"Yes, it's me. Can I come in?"

"Of course," Mimi said.

Chloe gasped when she saw Mimi. She knew her granddaughter was a beauty, but she had not anticipated just how breathtaking Mimi would look in her new blue dress with just a slight lipstick stain coloring her lips and cheeks a faint shade of red.

"You are so gorgeous!" Chloe exclaimed as her hands flew up to her cheeks.

"I look just like you, *Bubbie.*" Mimi laughed.

"You were right about that dress. It fits like it was made for you and that shade of blue sets off your eyes," Chloe said. She stood up. "Wait right here. I have something I want you to wear to the dance. It's something that means a lot to me."

"What is it, *Bubbie*?"

"You'll see." Chloe smiled as she walked into her bedroom. She opened the small jewelry box she had received as a gift from her mother when she was a child. It was a tiny music box. Inside she kept everything she had of value: a love letter from Max when he was in the army; her grandmother's embroidered handkerchief; and the brooch. Chloe closed her eyes as she lifted the pin and held it in her hand. The gold felt cool against her skin. In her mind's eye she saw Lily smiling at her. "Until we meet again," she heard Lily whisper. Then she felt Max's fingers brush her cheek. A single tear fell from her eye as she stood up and went back into the living room where Mimi waited. "I want you to wear this brooch. It means a lot to me."

"I'd forgotten how beautiful it is *Bubbie*," Mimi gasped.

"Yes, it is," Chloe said. "Will you wear it?"

"Of course. I would be honored to wear it."

"Good." Chloe smiled and she reached up and touched Mimi's hair. "In case you didn't know, you're the light of my life," she said as they hugged each other. "Someday this pin will be yours."

"I will cherish it more than anything else in the world," Mimi said.

"There will be so many things in life that you will cherish much more. Like your husband, your children, your home. It's a very pretty piece of jewelry, but it is only a brooch."

"I don't think I'll ever get married or have children," Mimi said wistfully. "Not after the way Nick treated me."

"Oh, my sweet girl," Chloe said as she took Mimi's hand and pulled her over to sit down on the bed beside her. "Nick was a nice boy, but he was only a childhood friend. Someday you will meet your husband, your *bashert*. Do you know what that means?"

"Sort of," Mimi said, staring into her grandmother's eyes.

"In Yiddish the word *bashert* means 'meant for you.' Anything that is meant for you is *bashert*. But when someone refers to 'your *bashert*', that means the person who God meant for you to share your life with."

"I don't think I have a *bashert*," Mimi said sadly. "I think I'm meant to spend my life alone."

"You're so young, Mimi. Give yourself a chance. You're still in school. Your adult life hasn't even begun yet."

"I'm almost finished with school, and I don't see any prospects for marriage in my future. In fact, I think since I'm going to be alone for the rest of my life, I'd like to teach school or work in the library to support myself."

"We'll see. Right now, you should be excited about going to your first dance, no?" Chloe winked at Mimi.

"Yes, you're right."

"Good. Now, I actually came into your room to let you know that Rose is here."

"How does she look?"

"Very pretty, and very excited." Chloe smiled.

"I can't wait to see her," Mimi said. "She is such a pretty girl. Sometimes I can't believe how tiny she is."

There isn't a selfish or competitive bone in Mimi's body, Chloe thought as she admired her granddaughter's kindness.

"Are you ready to go to the dance?" Chloe asked.

"Yes, *Bubbie*. I'm ready to leave."

"Would you like me to walk you two girls to the *shul*? It's getting dark outside," Chloe said, trying to hide the fear in her voice. Two young girls walking alone in the evening with everything going on in the world frightened her terribly.

"No, I don't want everyone to think I'm a baby," Mimi said. "It will be alright. Rose and I will be careful, and we'll be walking together."

"How about when you come home? Shall I meet you at the *shul* at ten o'clock?" Chloe said; she was conscious of not overstepping that delicate line between giving independence and clinging too tightly.

"No, *Bubbie*. I promise we'll be very careful walking home. We'll walk quickly and not talk to any strangers on the way. I promise."

"Well, once the two of you arrive here, you and I can walk Rose home together. That way she won't have to be out in the dark alone."

"Please don't worry, *Bubbie*. Rose's older brother is coming to the dance. He'll walk us home and then he'll walk her home, too."

"Very well. But I'll wait up for you."

"Yes, *Bubbie*," Mimi said, smiling.

Rose stood up when Mimi entered the room. The two girls began to jump up and down and hug each other. "You look beautiful," Rose said.

"So do you."

"I'm so excited. This is going to be so much fun."

"Yes, it will be," Mimi said, but Chloe could see in Mimi's eyes that she wasn't as excited about the dance as Rose was.

"Michael, my brother, is looking forward to finally meeting you. I've told him so much about you," Rose said. "He had to go to the *shul* early so he's already there. The sisterhood is setting up the dance, but they needed some of the boys to help with the heavier stuff. He volunteered; that's why he can't walk there with us."

"I'm looking forward to meeting him, too," Mimi said, smiling.

Chloe watched her granddaughter's face, and she could see that although Mimi was smiling, her smile never reached her eyes.

"Alright, you two. The dance has already begun and you're late," Chloe said.

"Goodbye, *Bubbie*. I'll see you at a little after ten tonight," Mimi said as she kissed her grandmother's cheek.

"Be careful, my love. You're very valuable to me." *Bubbie* always said this same phrase whenever she and Mimi were parting.

The girls left Mimi's apartment, walking quickly until they

arrived at the synagogue. Almost as soon as they entered, Rose's brother came over to them and introduced himself to Mimi.

"Hi, I'm Michael, it's nice to finally meet you—my sister has told me so much about you."

"This is my brother," Rose said.

"Nice to meet you. I'm Mimi," Mimi responded.

Michael was a pleasant-looking fellow with a warm smile, dark, wavy hair, and dark eyes like his sister. He wore a navy-blue suit and tie with a white shirt. He took Rose and Mimi's arms and said, "Let me escort you both over to the room where the dance is taking place."

Mimi smiled at Michael; she could tell that he liked her. He led the girls down a flight of stairs.

"I can't wait to see the faces of all the fellas when I walk in with the two of you beautiful girls," Michael said, smiling as he looked at Mimi.

The dance was taking place in a large room in the basement of the synagogue that was always used for private parties as well as events that were sponsored by the temple. It wasn't a fancy space, but it was very clean.

The floor was made of old, scuffed blond wood that had been recently washed and polished. The walls had been painted a stark white. Each week a maid came to the *shul* to dust the room and wash the floors.

There was a small dance floor at the front of the room, and several couples were dancing to a band, who played on a slightly raised stage, that was composed of some of the musically inclined members of the synagogue. At the back of the room stood a row of chairs where a half-dozen girls sat looking at their shoes and waiting to be asked to dance.

The lamps were covered with sheer pink scarves to soften the lighting. On the other side of the room, a long table covered with a clean white tablecloth had been set up with several platters of cookies and slices of cake. At the end of the table there was a large bowl filled with punch.

Michael saw Mimi eyeing the table. "The women from the sisterhood did a real nice job, don't you think? They baked everything over there," he said, smiling.

"Yes, it's quite lovely. It must have been a lot of work on their part," Mimi replied.

"Can I get you something? Punch? Cookies? I think Silvia Greenspan baked her famous *mandelbrot*. And Lila Blumenthal made strudel."

Mimi shook her head.

"Maybe a slice of cake?" Michael asked.

"Oh no, thank you. I'm not very hungry," she replied, suddenly feeling nervous.

"Well then, would you care to dance?" Michael asked Mimi.

Just then Lila Blumenthal, one of the women from the sisterhood, interrupted their conversation to ask Michael to help with some of the band's equipment that was not working properly. Mimi went over to a table where Rose sat with some other girls from school.

For a while, Mimi sat watching the dancers whirl around the dance floor. Some of them were graceful and fun to watch, while others could barely move around. Rose was asked to dance by a young man from school and she obliged. She smiled as she danced past Mimi. Mimi returned her smile. *Rose looks so happy*, Mimi thought.

Mimi was sat quietly watching couples dance to slow songs and some more upbeat tempos when a man walked over to her.

"I love the color of your dress," he said. "It's my favorite shade of blue. Now, most people, I believe, are partial to the shade sky blue, but to me, sky blue is too light. I prefer a more vivid color like the color of your dress. And, if I may be so bold, your dress matches your eyes perfectly: your eyes are the most remarkable shade I've ever seen."

Mimi looked up to see Michael standing beside her.

He just smiled and said, "I didn't really get a moment to talk to you with my sister standing next to us. I hope it's alright that I noticed your incredible eyes the minute you walked in here. You speak French with a beautiful accent. Are you British?" He was smiling brightly.

"American," she answered, looking up at him. Now that she had a moment to study Michael, she noticed that he was taller than most of the boys at the dance. But he was lanky, not filled out the way Nick had been. She cursed herself for comparing every boy she met to Nick. Michael had an easy smile. She smiled back at him and said, "But I came to live in France when I was young."

"I must be honest with you. I'm rather surprised that you aren't up dancing every dance. I mean, after all, anyone can see that you're the prettiest girl here."

Mimi laughed and shook her head. "That's not true."

"Oh, but it is," he said, smiling.

She laughed again, unsure what to say.

"Can I get you a glass of punch?" he asked.

Until Michael mentioned a drink, Mimi had not realized that she was thirsty. "Yes, actually, I would like that."

"Don't move. I'll be right back," he said.

Mimi watched Michael fill two small glasses with the ladle by the punch bowl and select a few cookies that he wrapped in a napkin. When he returned, he handed her one of the glasses and offered her a cookie. "I brought some refreshments in case you were hungry."

"Thank you," she said sincerely, taking one of the cookies and nibbling on it.

"May I sit down?" he asked. "Or perhaps you might like to dance?"

Mimi could see that he was nervous and was trying hard to make conversation with her.

"I'm not really in the mood to dance right now. Why don't you sit down and perhaps we can have a dance in a little while?" she suggested.

Michael sat down beside her, and she felt the heat of his body next to hers. It made her uncomfortable. "I'm sorry. I'm just not very good at these things. I would much rather stay at home and read. I'm afraid I don't do well in social settings," she admitted.

"It's alright. Neither do I. I'd much prefer to be at home with my cat," he said, smiling at her.

"You have a cat? Rose never mentioned that," she said excitedly.

"Of course? What's life if you don't have a cat?"

"I don't have one."

"Well, we'll have to fix that now, won't we?"

"My grandmother would not be too happy if I got a pet. We can hardly afford to feed ourselves."

He smiled at her. "I want to be a veterinarian. I love animals and it's my dream to care for them. There's a veterinary college in Lyon. I plan to attend next year."

"Is it a difficult program?" Mimi asked. Michael had piqued her interest and she wanted to know more about him.

"From what I hear, it is. But it's my passion. What's yours?"

She had never really thought about it. Now that he mentioned it, she felt like she needed to give it some serious consideration. "I don't know really. I study ballet and I enjoy it very much. My grandmother is my teacher; she was a ballerina. She's so elegant and graceful, I would love to be more like her. But the truth is, ballet is her passion. Not mine really. I don't know what my passion is. Perhaps I don't have one." Mimi shrugged her shoulders.

"I'm sure you do. Don't be too concerned, I know you'll figure it out. Maybe your passion is to have a home, a husband, children. Motherhood is a very important career," Michael said. "It might just be the most important career a woman can have."

Mimi sighed. There was a time when she believed that Nick would come back into her life, and they would get married and raise a family. *How silly that was of me,* she thought sadly. *Bubbie is right, Nick and I were just children when we made those vows. How can I even think there was any truth to them? Now, he's all grown up and so am I. How could I ever believe we would still be close and still have anything in common?*

"Since you've studied dance, I would love to dance with you. Are you willing to give me one dance?" Michael asked humbly.

"Alright," Mimi said, nodding. She put her empty cup on a small table and followed him to the dance floor. He took her hand in his and she felt a spark of electricity run through her. They began to dance. Michael was a good dancer; he was graceful and considerate. When the music ended, they began to sway to another song.

"Did your grandmother teach you to dance like this or did she only teach you ballet?"

"She gave Rose and me a quick course in ballroom dancing before we came to this party."

"Well, you can tell her that you glide across the floor just like a professional." He smiled. "You move so beautifully in my arms."

She couldn't help but smile.

Mimi and Michael waltzed and then did a foxtrot, and continued as the band played several more tunes before he said, "How about another glass of punch? Are you thirsty?"

"I am," she said.

"I'll be right back."

They whirled around the floor in each other's arms until the clock read five minutes to ten and the band announced that they were about to play the last song.

THIRTY-EIGHT

Rose was waiting at the door for Mimi when she arrived with Michael at her side. The three of them began to walk in the direction of their apartments. The streets were busier than they expected. There seemed to be a lot of commotion, but the three young adults were distracted by the excitement of their evening.

"I just had the best night." Rose turned to Mimi. "Did you see that Ezra, the rabbi's son, asked me to dance? I hope he wants to see me again."

"I did," Mimi said, trying to match Rose's happiness. Then she looked at Michael and when her eyes caught his, she felt a flush of red come to her face.

In a soft voice, Michael whispered to Mimi, "I know you're very busy, but do you think you could make some time to have an ice cream with a fellow?" He winked. "Me being that fellow."

She laughed. "I suppose I could."

"How about tomorrow? What time do you get home from school and when is your dance class?"

"I don't have a class tomorrow, but I'll be home from school at four."

"Perfect, I'll come over and pick you up and we can go and have an ice cream together."

Michael took Mimi's hand and held it for a moment. She smiled at him as they turned the corner of her street. Rose was giggling and beaming with delight as she rambled on about her dance with Ezra. They were a few feet from Mimi's apartment when Michael bent down to kiss Mimi, but just as his lips were about to touch hers, a woman who lived across the street came running up to them. There was a nasty cut on her face which had dripped blood on to her white blouse. Her face was flushed, and she was shaking.

"There's a demonstration against Jews going on in town," she said. "Wild boys are running around beating people with sticks. Someone threw a rock through the window of the dance studio. I was on my way to tell your grandmother about it, but I saw you and—"

"Oh, my goodness!" Michael said. "Is your grandmother at the studio or at home?" he asked Mimi.

"I don't know. It's late so I expect she's at home, but she may have gone in to see Maurice." Mimi felt her heartbeat quicken. She had to find her grandmother and Maurice now.

"Come. Let's go now," Michael said hurriedly as they all flew down the street.

When Mimi, Michael, and Rose entered the apartment panting and breathless, Chloe noticed the panicked look on Mimi's face. "What's wrong? What's going on?" she asked.

Mimi told her grandmother everything their neighbor had said. Chloe's hand began to shake as she covered her mouth. "Dear God," she whispered. "Maurice was working late tonight. He was setting up the studio for the recital tomorrow. I must go to him."

Michael put his hand on Chloe's arm. "It could be dangerous. You stay here with Mimi and Rose. I'll go."

THIRTY-NINE

Michael made his way through the streets to the dance studio to check on Maurice. He passed by men, women, and children who were wounded and bleeding.

Women were kneeling over bodies screaming and crying, but Michael had to stay focused. As he walked towards the studio, he saw that a crowd had gathered in front of the building. When he got closer, he saw that the front window of the studio was smashed. There was glass everywhere. Someone had entered the studio and painted red swastikas over the walls. *"Juden"* was written in the same red paint.

This was horrifying but not nearly as horrifying as what Michael saw next. Maurice's body was lying in the center of the room. He was dead, lying still on the floor in a pool of dried blood. Michael felt his heart pounding as bile rose in his throat.

Maurice's head had been bashed in and his beautiful, kind face was destroyed.

He knelt beside him and took Maurice's hand, noticing that the front of his white shirt was soaked with red blood. *How am I ever going to tell Mimi, Chloe, and my sister what has happened here? It will destroy them. They loved Maurice. He was such a good and kind man. How could anyone be so cruel?*

FORTY

Mimi thought she would lose her mind. The hours ticked by and still Michael did not return.

"What if something happened to him?" Rose asked. "I'm worried. Maybe I should go and try to find him? Or maybe I should go home and tell my father, and he can go?"

"No, you must not go out. You should stay here and wait with us," Chloe said. "We don't know what's happening out there and you can't risk it."

Rose did not ask again; she just stared out the window while Mimi and Chloe sat on the sofa on either side of her.

The sun was just rising when there was a knock on the door. The three women, wide-eyed and frightened, stared at each other before Chloe stood up and looked through the peephole. "It's Michael," she said as she flung the door open.

Mimi gasped when she saw him. His eye was bruised and turning purple. There was a gash on his chin that was bleeding profusely and his shirt was torn. His hands were filthy with blood and she knew he had been caught up in the violence. "Michael," she said. "What happened?"

"There's a gang of thugs in the street. They've gone wild. They're beating people up. It's total chaos. The police are there but they aren't doing anything to stop it." He was breathless from fighting.

Mimi got up and went into the bathroom where she retrieved a clean towel. Then she filled a bowl with warm water and began to clean Michael's wounds. Rose was biting her nails.

"Michael," Chloe said hesitantly. "Did you see Maurice?"

Michael took Mimi's hand in his and for a moment he stopped her from dressing his wounds. "Yes," he said solemnly.

"Is he alright? Is the studio alright?" Chloe asked.

"No," Michael said, looking down at the floor. "I was too late to help him. I'm sorry."

"What do you mean?" Chloe asked, her voice almost hysterical.

"They killed him. They vandalized the studio, and they murdered him."

"Oh my God," Chloe said. "Maurice. Why Maurice? He was such a good man."

Mimi began to weep. Michael took her into his arms and she cried on his shoulder. It was at that moment that she realized she was falling in love with him.

Chloe shrugged, her eyes brimming with tears. "I'm sure it was the Nazis, but why did they choose Maurice? He never hurt anyone in his life."

"I know why. They didn't target Maurice; they wanted to kill Jews. They want us to be miserable," Michael said angrily. "They did it because we're Jewish. It's as simple as that. They hate Jews."

"But why choose Maurice? He wasn't political in any way," Mimi said.

"He was Jewish, popular, well-liked, and an open homosexual," Michael said. "I've read a lot about the Nazis since they began invading our neighboring countries and they hate Jews and homosexuals. They hate other groups, too, but especially Jews. Maurice was just the sort of person they wanted to use to make an example."

"This is just so horrible," Mimi said, shaking her head.

"Yes, it is," Michael replied.

"I hate to leave France because I love it. But in these circumstances, I think we should try to get out of Europe as soon as we possibly can. We should try to get to America or anywhere else far from here," Chloe said.

"I don't speak English. In fact, I don't speak anything except French and Latin," Michael said. "How will I go to university if we go to America?"

"I don't know," Chloe said. "I don't know what to do, but we must find some way to get out of Europe."

The funeral was a dark and solemn day for Chloe. Maurice had been her best friend for many years and now he was gone. She would have contacted Maurice's family, but he had told her that they had disowned him because of his sexuality, so she didn't try.

Chloe, Mimi, Rose, Michael, and a few of Maurice's friends stood in front of the newly dug grave along with a handful of students from the studio who came to pay their respects. The rabbi spoke, but Chloe hardly heard him. The voices in her head were screaming too loud. They were telling her to get her family out of Europe as soon as possible.

After the funeral service, Chloe walked back home. She was broken. Even the warm sunlight on her shoulders could not lift her spirits. She was devastated at the loss of her best friend and terrified about what the future might hold for her precious granddaughter.

When Chloe received a telephone call from Maurice's lawyer letting her know that Maurice had left the dance studio to her in his will, she cried with tears of joy and great sadness. It was so bittersweet. "I don't know what to do," she said to Michael and Mimi. "I can't bear the thought of leaving Paris. Now that the studio belongs to me, it's even more difficult because I feel obligated to the students. But I know we can't stay here. It's getting too dangerous."

"I know the studio means so much to everyone," Mimi replied sadly.

"Yes, when it belonged to Maurice, I felt alright about leaving because I knew he'd take care of the students," Chloe said. "But if I go now, I'll smash all their dreams."

"You could sell it," Michael suggested.

"To whom? It's a Jewish-owned business. I don't think anyone would buy it," Chloe said. "Besides, I doubt that Maurice would want me to do that."

"So let's take our chances and stay," Mimi said. "This is France. The French people will not let the Germans torture the French Jews. They will stand up for us."

"I agree with Mimi," Michael said.

Chloe nodded, but she wasn't convinced.

Mimi put her hand on her *bubbie's* shoulder reassuringly. "Then it's been decided. We'll stick it out here," Mimi said. "Dance classes will go on as they always have and there will be recitals. We'll do all of this in poor Maurice's honor. Our dear friend, Maurice. What a good person he was. Whoever did this to him has robbed the world of a very special man."

"I couldn't agree more. He was a very good person," Michael said.

"He was like a father to me," Mimi said.

FORTY-ONE

Chloe had just gotten home from her day of work at the dance studio when Mimi returned from the market. Chloe was about to go into the kitchen to prepare a stew for dinner when she looked up and saw the anxious look on Mimi's face. "What is it? What's happened? What's wrong?" she asked. "Did you go to see Michael?"

"Oh, *Bubbie*, I might be crazy. I mean, it's all so soon," Mimi said.

"Sit down on the sofa. Let's have a talk. You're not making sense. I don't know what you're talking about." Chloe sat down beside her granddaughter and took Mimi's hands in hers. She looked into Mimi's eyes.

Mimi returned her grandmother's gaze and said, "I think I'm in love with Michael. With everything that's happened to us, he's been such a comfort. I just don't want to get hurt."

Chloe took a long deep breath and said, "Life will hurt you sometimes, my little one. I know that love can be painful, but it's all part of living. When you find your *bashert*, the boy who is meant for you, it will all be worth it. I know you're young, but you know what you feel. Ask yourself honestly, do you think it might be Michael?"

"I do, *Bubbie*. I believe it's him." Mimi shivered. "I wish I could just be a child forever. Growing up is so scary. What if I make the wrong decision? I believe that Michael is my *bashert*, but I used to think Nick was my *bashert*. How will I know if I'm making the right choice?"

"I know it's scary," Chloe said as Mimi collapsed into her arms.

Tears fell down Mimi's cheeks. "I just don't want to get hurt again."

Mimi lay quietly sobbing on her *bubbie's* shoulder for almost a quarter of an hour before they were disturbed by a loud knock on the door.

Chloe whispered to Mimi, "Stay right here, it's probably one of the students. I know this is a tough time for you, so I'll tell them to come back tomorrow." She stood up and walked to the door. Before Chloe looked through the peephole she muttered, "Who is it?"

"It's Michael. I know I probably shouldn't have come over unannounced, but I need to speak to Mimi. Please can you open the door?"

Chloe turned to look at Mimi. She whispered in a voice just loud enough for Mimi to hear, "Can I let him in? Or would you rather I didn't?"

Mimi threw her hands up. "I don't know what to do!"

"Please, let me in. I just need to speak to Mimi for a few minutes," Michael begged.

Mimi wiped the tears off her face with her sweater sleeve and whispered, "Let him in, *Bubbie*."

Chloe opened the door to find an out-of-breath, red-faced Michael on the doorstep. She realized that he had been running.

"Mimi," he said, rushing over to where Mimi was sitting on the sofa. He knelt beside her. "I haven't been able to sleep or eat. I ran all the way to your apartment because I wanted to get here as quickly as possible. I have something I have to tell you, and it can't wait—"

"What is it? Is everything alright?" Mimi asked, looking at him curiously.

"Mimi," he said in a low and serious voice. "I've realized that I love you. I really love you and I'm sure that you are my *bashert*. Do you know what that means?"

"Yes, actually, I do," she said. Tears began to flow down her cheeks again.

"Why are you crying?" Michael asked.

"Because," she hesitated, "because I love you, too."

He put his arms around her and kissed her. "Marry me, Mimi. I want to get married as soon as possible. With everything that's happening in the country right now, I don't want to hesitate. Let's get married as soon as you finish school. I'll apply to the closest university so we can stay here in Paris. That way you can stay close to your *bubbie*. I know how much she means to you, and I don't want to take you away from her."

"But what if my *bubbie* and I decide to leave France?" Mimi asked.

"Then we'll all leave together. I'll change universities if I have to. I want you to be my wife. What do you say? Will you marry me?"

She nodded. "Yes, yes, I'll marry you."

Michael threw his arms around Mimi and kissed her. "I'm going to make you so happy," he said. "I'll be the best husband ever."

Chloe didn't want to interrupt their special moment, but she turned to look at them both and said, "I want to let you know that I'm going to stay in Paris. At least for now. So many dance students depend on our studio, and I don't want to leave them without a place to study. If you want to get married, I'm all for it. After Michael is finished with university, we'll decide whether to leave Paris or not. Hopefully by then, this hatred towards Jewish people will have fizzled out."

"I am very happy that we have your blessing," Michael said to Chloe. "It means a lot to me, and I know it means a lot to Mimi."

"I have to admit, I feel a little uneasy because you're both so young," Chloe said. "But the truth is, you're no younger than I was when I married my husband, Max—may his memory always be a blessing. We were very happy together."

"Does that mean that you approve, *Bubbie?*" Mimi asked eagerly.

"If this makes you happy, then yes, I approve, and you both have my blessings."

Mimi stood up and ran over to her grandmother. "Thank you, *Bubbie.*"

Chloe hugged Mimi tightly. "I will do anything I can for the two of you, because now, Michael, you are like family to me."

Michael stood up and walked over to Chloe and Mimi. Chloe turned and pulled him towards her. "This," she said, "requires a toast." She took a half-empty bottle of wine off the shelf, poured three small glasses, and handed one to Michael and one to Mimi. Chloe took her glass and smiled. She raised it and said, "To a bright future for two very warm and special young people."

They clinked their glasses and drank.

FORTY-TWO

Mimi had finished school and had also taken a course in typing and shorthand. Now that she had completed her education, Mimi and Michael began to discuss plans for their upcoming wedding ceremony with Chloe and Rose.

"I think it's too hot to for us to plan a party like this in late summer. All the ladies' dresses will stick to them with sweat," Rose said, laughing. "You know how women are when it comes to their clothes, everyone wants to look like they're at the height of fashion. That might be rather difficult if it's blisteringly hot outside. The curls will fall from their hair and their makeup will run. Besides, what about Mimi and her gown? It would be unbearable for her to wear a heavy dress in the middle of summer. No, no." Rose sighed. "In my opinion, the best time for the wedding is in autumn. It's such a beautiful time of year. What do you two think?" she asked.

Rose was always one to think of everything. Since Michael and Rose's family was paying for the wedding, it seemed only right for it to take place during autumn if that was what they wanted.

Chloe watched her granddaughter's face as Mimi looked at Michael. There was no doubt in Chloe's mind that Mimi was in love.

"I love autumn," Mimi said. "But Michael and I are so ready to get married. I mean, if it were up to us, we would forgo having a wedding and just get married without a celebration. It seems like we've been engaged and waiting forever. Although I understand why you wanted us to spend time together to make sure we were making the right decision, *Bubbie*," Mimi said, addressing her grandmother.

"Your grandmother is a smart lady. Marriage is a very important commitment," Rose said. She winked at Chloe who smiled at her.

"I love the idea of an autumn wedding, and the weather should still be nice in October," Chloe said. She really liked Michael. The more she got to know him the more she saw him as a grandson. Even so, marriage was a big step, and she was nervous about Mimi starting this new stage of her life. However, she was glad that Mimi and Michael had agreed to live with her after the wedding until he finished his studies at university. This would give her more time with her cherished granddaughter.

"My family has a very good friend who will do the catering for us. His fee is reasonable and his food is exquisite," Rose said, smiling, but Chloe was hardly listening.

Chloe was thinking about how much things would change once Mimi was married. It had been a sort of utopia for Chloe since Mimi had come into her life. She had never stopped missing or loving her daughter, but Lily was gone and so she poured all the love she had in her heart into Mimi. Chloe let out a long sigh.

"Are you alright?" Rose asked.

"Oh yes, of course. I'm just a little tired. My age is getting to me," Chloe said. "I wish Maurice were here. It would have meant so much to him to see you get married."

"I miss him, too, *Bubbie*," Mimi said. "I would have let him give me away if he were here."

"He would have *kvelled*. He loved you so, Mimi."

"I know, *Bubbie*. I loved him, too," Mimi replied gently. Her eyes were misty with tears.

"So did I."

Mimi got up and walked to the window. She turned her face away from everyone and stared outside for a long time.

Chloe wondered if Mimi was thinking about Nick. After all, the last they had heard from Nick was that he was living in Berlin. Gloria had told Chloe that her husband, Friedrich, was a member of the Nazi party. As Friedrich had adopted Nick and was very close to him, Chloe wondered if they were both involved with the Nazi atrocities in Germany and beyond. *I wonder if Mimi ever told Michael about Nick?* Chloe thought. *Does Michael know the story of Mimi's parents and how Gloria and Nick brought her here to France? Or perhaps Mimi didn't see any reason to tell Michael about Nick—maybe he's little more than a memory for her now.*

FORTY-THREE
AUTUMN 1941

After putting on her wedding dress, Mimi sat down on the window ledge and looked outside. The leaves were just beginning to turn beautiful hues of amber and russet, and some of them had fallen to the ground. However, her once-beautiful view of her Parisian street had now been tainted with bright-red Nazi flags hanging from the windows.

Considering the political climate and the fear spreading through France, Mimi and Michael had assumed that most of their guests would not attend their wedding anyway. Things were becoming increasingly difficult for Jews each day. Many of Mimi and Chloe's friends had lost their jobs or their businesses. Mimi felt a flash of anxiety every time she passed a newsstand because the newspapers had begun to feature blatant and offensive propaganda against Jews.

"Perhaps we should just cancel the wedding and get married at the courthouse," Mimi suggested. "With the German invasion, I doubt anyone will attend anyway."

"Nonsense," Chloe said determinedly. "The only way to fight against this Nazi machine is to embrace whatever joy we can find. After all, we are French, and this is the way the French do things.

There's no reason to cancel the wedding. I'm sure the guests will try to make it if they can. You two lovebirds will be married and live happily ever after." But even as Chloe said them, her words felt hollow. Their lives were consumed with fear and suffering, Chloe wanted to believe that a celebration for Mimi and Michael would bring some light into the dark world they were living in.

Chloe smiled at Mimi, but her lips were quivering. Her intuition told her that something terrible was on the horizon, and because of this she found herself unable to sleep or eat. However, she refused to put a damper on her granddaughter's joy, so she kept her fears to herself.

As expected, several guests did not attend the wedding. Even so, it was a beautiful ceremony conducted under a *chuppah*, a canopy made of four wooden posts covered in white tulle. The local reformed rabbi performed a heartfelt ceremony. Mimi was stunning in the white satin gown that Chloe and Rose helped her pick out.

Chloe had purchased the dress at an elegant boutique owned by a friend of Maurice. The dress was very expensive, but the owner knew that Maurice had been close to Mimi, so he insisted that Chloe buy the dress at a discounted price. "She was like a daughter to Maurice, and he was such a wonderful friend to me," the shop owner had said. "He would have wanted to make sure that Mimi's wedding was perfect. It's the least I can do."

As she walked beside Mimi, Chloe looked elegant, tall, and graceful in a dark-blue dress that accented her eyes. Tears welled as she directed her granddaughter under the canopy where Michael stood waiting for her. Michael was tall and proud, looking refined and handsome in a black suit. And even though food was scarce, the meal turned out to be better than expected. The wedding took place in the studio and the band played well into the night.

. . .

After the wedding ended and the guests left, Chloe and Rose stayed behind to begin cleaning up the dance studio. Once they had finished, they walked towards home together. They walked quietly, careful to stay in the shadows and not attract any attention from the German soldiers who were now scattered like ants across the city.

"We're married," Michael whispered to Mimi as they entered her bedroom.

"Yes, we are," Mimi said, smiling. She was a virgin and very nervous. It seemed strange for Michael to be in her room. *I hope this isn't going to hurt, and I really hope Michael is my bashert*, she thought. *I believe he is. But how can I know for sure?*

Michael didn't rush her. He was a tender and considerate lover and once the first time was over Mimi found that she enjoyed making love with Michael. It made her feel closer to him than she had ever thought possible. They were so wrapped up in each other that they hardly slept that night. As Mimi lay in Michael's arms, she felt safe for the moment, but she couldn't help but wonder what their future would look like.

"Michael." Mimi looked up and her husband's eyes met hers.

"Yes, my wife," he replied playfully.

"Michael, I'm scared," Mimi responded. Her voice was serious. "I want children, but how can we think about children with the Nazis threatening our every move?"

He pulled her in closer. "Mimi, I vowed to love and protect you, and I will always do that. You are my world now. I will protect you and all of our future children with my life." Michael leaned down and kissed her, Mimi returned his kiss. He continued, "This won't last forever. The Nazis will be gone before you know it, and we'll have a big, beautiful family to fill even the biggest room with laughter and love." Michael kissed her again, and Mimi melted into his arms.

As the sun began to rise, they both fell asleep, exhausted and spent.

FORTY-FOUR

UKRAINE, 1941

Up until now, Nick had been lucky, and he had not seen combat. He always assumed that Friedrich had pulled some strings and therefore he had managed to avoid it. With no previous fighting experience, he was not particularly concerned when the army sent him and his platoon on a special assignment to Ukraine. Although Nick had no idea what kind of job he was being sent to carry out, he was not worried about it. Before he left Germany, he was given a few days of leave, so he went to see his parents.

Friedrich and Gloria were so happy to have Nick home that they hosted a dinner party in his honor. Friedrich invited several important party members and everyone made a fuss over Nick; they all said that he looked handsome in his uniform. When Nick entered the ballroom at the back of Friedrich's estate, two very pretty young women who he did not recognize were sitting at a table in the back of the room. Friedrich introduced the girls to Nick and they both fawned over him. At first, he seemed to enjoy the attention, but he soon grew distracted and made excuses to go and talk to the other guests.

"Didn't you like those girls?" Friedrich asked him.

"They were very nice, but not really my type," Nick said.

"I was hoping one of them would catch your interest. They're both from good families. Their fathers have good positions in the party."

"Yes, they told me," Nick said flatly.

"Eventually, it would be good for you to get married. The sooner the better," Friedrich said. "A marriage to a girl from the right background is good for your career."

"Yes, Father. So you and Mother keep telling me. However, I've yet to meet anyone who strikes my fancy."

"Marriage doesn't have to be a love story, Nick. All you need is to marry the right girl. A pure Aryan girl with good breeding. You bring her with you when you meet important people, and she will be an asset. Then you have a couple of beautiful children and you'll have it made. The Führer believes in good German family values. He wants our pure Aryan young people to have plenty of children. With your looks and your family background, who knows how high you can rise?"

"Yes, I suppose so," Nick said. "I know it's hard to believe, Father, but I'm still a hopeless romantic."

Friedrich let out a laugh. "Romance fades, son. Good bloodlines don't. If, after you're married, you still need romance, then you can find a little bit on the side. You know what I mean?"

"You never did that," Nick said, hoping he was right. "Did you, Father?"

"I was lucky. I happened to meet and marry a girl who I love very much," Friedrich lied, realizing that he had probably said too much already. He never wanted Nick to see him in a bad light. It was true that he had been madly in love with Gloria in the beginning, but that had all ended years ago. Although he hoped Nick would never find out, Friedrich had been having extra-marital affairs ever since.

Nick's time on leave passed very quickly. In what seemed like the blink of an eye, he was standing in the train station where he would meet up with a group of other German soldiers and they would all board a train headed to Ukraine.

As usual, the station was crowded but Nick finally boarded the train and took a seat by the window. The whistle blew and then the train rocked a little on the rails and came to life. It chugged along with a sweet rhythmic motion that made Nick feel relaxed and tired.

He tried to resist the urge to sleep but finally drifted off with his head against the window. He dreamt of Mimi. In his mind's eye he saw her face. It had been years since he thought of her. She was a twelve-year-old child looking up to him for words of wisdom and guidance.

In his dream, Mimi did not speak, but when he got close to her, he could see that she was crying. Nick wished he could tell her something that would ease her pain.

Someone in the train car laughed loudly and jolted Nick from his dream. He woke to find himself sitting next to a man in his early twenties. He realized that he must have drifted off for a few stops because now he was surrounded by a small platoon of German soldiers. They were not men from his regular platoon. In fact, he didn't recognize any of them, but they seemed to know each other because they were talking among themselves like old friends.

Men in military uniforms often formed an instant bond so it was difficult to tell whether they really knew each other or they had just become friends. One of the soldiers smiled at Nick. Nick nodded and returned his smile. He glanced out of the window. "Where are we?" Nick asked loudly.

One of the soldiers replied, "I think we're about to enter Ukraine."

Nick nodded. "Thank you. Does anyone know what our mission is here?" he asked. "Are we expecting to go to battle?"

If they knew, no one volunteered an answer. Nick settled back against the train car wall watching the countryside roll past. He had no idea that within hours he was going to be forced to participate in a mission that would haunt him for the rest of his life.

FORTY-FIVE

BABI YAR, UKRAINE, SEPTEMBER 30, 1941

When the soldiers stepped off the train, their faces were assaulted by an icy wind. It could get cold in Germany, but this was a different cold. A shiver ran down Nick's spine and he pulled his scarf tighter around his neck as he gathered into a group surrounded by the rest of the soldiers.

A few minutes later, an open-air army truck arrived and Nick, along with the other soldiers, climbed on to the back. Someone started to sing a familiar German folk song and several of the others joined in. Nick was too cold to sing. He was looking out at the rural landscape and wishing he was comfortably back at home in Berlin.

In the distance Nick could see a long line of people with frightened eyes. They were carrying suitcases. As the truck moved closer, it seemed that the line stretched for miles. The people were not soldiers. There were men, but there were also women and young children. They appeared to be ordinary citizens. He wondered if they were displaced persons who the army had been sent to relocate.

Nick noticed that everyone who stood in the line wore the yellow Star of David that indicated they were Jewish. Seeing this, he assumed that he was right, they were being moved. The Jews were surrounded by armed guards and Nick could see that they were being forced to walk. These people were not being relocated of their own free will.

The soldiers surrounding them were preoccupied, laughing and talking amongst themselves. They paid no attention to the Jews. Even the soldiers on the truck were engaged in conversations, seemingly unaware of the long line of people. But Nick was aware, and he was on edge. Some of the soldiers tried to include him in their chats, but he sat quietly. He had a sick feeling in the pit of his stomach, a feeling he could not explain.

He closed his eyes and remembered that the Jews were not human, they were *untermenschen. That's what they said about the Jews at every meeting that Father and I attended,* Nick thought. *Although I keep telling myself that they're only Jews, I can't murder them. When I look at them, they look like human beings. They bleed like human beings and when I think of shooting and killing them, I can't escape the horror of it. Their terrified eyes haunt me. Killing in battle is bad enough, but killing women and children, even if they are Jews, is something I cannot bear.*

When the truck reached the front of the line, Nick was close enough to see the frightened look on the faces of the Jews. He jumped when he heard a round of gunshots. The sound silenced the rest of the soldiers on the slowly moving truck. Less than a hundred feet in front of them was a deep ravine. This was where the truck stopped.

"Alright, we're here. Let's go," the general said sternly. "Get off the truck, we have a lot of work to do."

Nick watched the ravine while he waited for his turn to jump down from the truck bed. What he saw left him speechless.

A soldier with a large gun led a group of Jewish men, women, and children away from the rest of the line who were not permitted to see where they would eventually be going. A little boy clung to his mother's neck, his thin body shaking with every sob. Nick felt something twist in his gut. The child reminded him of himself at that age—burrowing into his mother's arms whenever he was frightened. Nick's throat was dry.

The Jews who had been led away from the rest were forced to line up at the edge of the ravine. Behind them, a group of German soldiers stood pointing their guns at the defenseless Jews. When the general in charge fired a shot, the other soldiers raised their guns and pointed them at the people who stood in front of them. Then they fired. Nick had to stifle a scream that rose in his throat. The little boy who, just a few minutes ago, had reminded Nick of himself as a child, was sheltered from the gunfire by his mother's lifeless body. Nick could hear the little boy screaming and wailing as his mother and the other Jews toppled like rag dolls into the ravine. The others were dead, but because the boy was screaming the soldiers knew he was still alive. So, one of them walked over to the edge of the ravine, pointed his gun, and shot the child. The small boy died instantly. Nick felt his vision blur before him. There was a roaring in his ears as he staggered away. In eerie silence, the rest of the soldiers snatched the suitcases that had belonged to the men, women, and children who now lay dead in the ravine and placed them in a pile on the other side of a copse of trees.

Before he was sent to Ukraine, Nick had prayed, begging God that his luck would hold out and he would not be sent into battle. But never in his life had he witnessed anything as hideous as this. This was not battle, this was cold-blooded murder. It was the murder of defenseless, unarmed people. *They're subhuman, Nick, less than animals*: Friedrich's words filled his head but as Nick took in the horrific scene before him, he could only see people—fathers, mothers, daughters, sons. He wondered if he would ever be able to get the image of that little boy and his mother out of his mind.

"Heil Hitler!" one of the high-ranking officers addressed the new arrivals, Nick among them.

"Heil Hitler!" the young soldiers who had just gotten off the truck replied in unison.

"Welcome to Babi Yar," the officer said. "This lovely ravine is actually the portal to hell." He smiled, amused by his own description. "You're going to find that what we're doing here is rather grueling work. However, it must be done. I'm sure that as you drove up you were able to see that our work is far from over. There is a long line of *untermenschen* waiting to be processed."

Waiting to be processed! Nick thought, appalled by the officer's language. *They are being forced to line up so they can be systematically killed.* He shuddered as a chill ran up his spine.

The officer continued, pointing at the firing squad, "You have been summoned here to give these soldiers who have been working tirelessly a bit of a break. So, that being said, get in line and prepare to shoot."

Prepare to shoot? Nick felt a cold sweat break out on his forehead.

The new arrivals glanced awkwardly at each other and then did as they were told. Nick stood in line beside a young man who appeared to be no more than eighteen. For a moment their eyes met. The officer began to speak again, "Now that you're ready for them, the next group of swine in need of processing will be lined up. When I give the order, you will shoot. Shoot to kill. Do you understand?"

"Yes, sir," the soldiers answered in unison.

"Anyone left standing or anyone who has not fallen into the gully will be assisted into the ravine by one of you. No one is to be left alive. Am I making myself clear? Everyone must be in the ravine when the next selection is brought forward."

"Yes, sir," they all answered.

Nick felt his fingers trembling on the trigger of his gun as a group of Jews was led to the edge of the ravine. He saw a man with long sideburns swaying back and forth as he prayed in a language Nick did not understand. A young girl stood alone; she was weeping. Nick's eyes scanned over those who were about to die. He was going to vomit. This was wrong: *terribly wrong.* He was desperately thinking of a way to excuse himself when the officer yelled out, "Fire."

Nick purposely aimed too high so he knew he would not hit his mark.

The soldiers fired. The smell of gunpowder assaulted his nose and gunfire shattered the quiet as the line of people fell.

The sound of a baby crying drifted up from the ravine. A soldier walked over to the edge of the ravine and pointed his gun at the infant, but the general said, "Don't bother. It's just a baby. Not worth the bullet. He'll die of starvation or he'll be smothered by bodies; if not, we'll bury him alive. Either way, he's just an infant so he can't get out."

As the next group was lining up, Nick looked over the edge of the ravine at the pile of dead bodies. The sight shook him, and he tried to avoid seeing their dark eyes staring back up at him. But then he saw another tiny infant. This one, he thought, was a girl, because she was wrapped in a pink winter coat with a matching hat. She was quiet, lying silently among the dead. Next to the child was a young woman with long dark hair. *She must be the baby's mother*, he thought. *The poor woman dressed her little one warmly this morning, not knowing or at least not believing that they were going to die today.*

The officer stood with his legs spread apart, his hands on his hips, watching Nick with a sense of curiosity. As the moments ticked away, he began to pace. He was losing his patience. He stopped and stared at Nick for a long moment before stomping his boot on the ground. "Shoot that child," he ordered.

Nick shook his head. He was unable to speak. His whole body trembled.

"Did you hear me?" the officer demanded. "I said, shoot the child. I would usually say don't waste the bullet, that it will die of starvation regardless, however the incessant crying is grating on my nerves. Shoot it to shut it up," he shouted.

"I can't," Nick said feebly. "I'm sorry. I just can't." The gun fell from his hands.

The officer glared at him and shook his head. "Don't tell me we have a weakling among us," he sneered. "You're Friedrich Wagner's son, aren't you? I thought you would have been a stronger person, but I can see you are weak."

"I'm sorry," Nick managed to choke.

The baby continued to cry, his wails echoing through the air.

"I said, shoot it. And you will."

Bile rose in Nick's throat and he vomited. "I'm sorry," he stammered.

The officer looked at him in disgust. He walked over to Nick and stood directly in front of him, so close that Nick could smell his foul *sauerkraut* breath. "Shoot the child right now and stop its infuriating wailing," he said. This time his voice was raised with anger.

Nick shook his head. "I can't."

"You will."

"No," Nick insisted.

The officer was hollering directly into Nick's face. "Shoot the child. Shoot it. Shoot it." He shook Nick's shoulders. "Get a hold of yourself. Perhaps I am wrong, perhaps you are not the son of Fredrick Wagner."

Nick said nothing.

"Well, are you or are you not his son?"

Nick nodded. "I am."

"Your father would be ashamed to have raised such a coward. You are nothing but a weak coward." The officer's eyes were on fire as he stared into Nick's eyes. "Shoot the child!" His voice was deep, raspy, and harsh. "Do it immediately or I'm going to be forced to send you for a mental evaluation."

Nick's hands shook as he stooped to pick up his gun.

The baby was still screaming.

The officer kept shouting, "Shoot the child!"

Nick pulled the trigger.

The screaming stopped. The infant was silent.

What have I done?

"You'll get used to it," the officer said. He seemed relieved as he patted Nick's shoulder. "We have a job to do, and we must do it."

Group after group of Jews lined up at the edge of the ravine until they were shot by the soldiers. As they fell, they filled the ravine with what seemed like a million dead bodies.

That evening when the soldiers sat down to eat, Nick couldn't take a single bite. He lay down and fell into a fitful sleep plagued with images of a crying baby.

In the middle of the night, he woke in a cold sweat. He sat up and looked around. The other soldiers were snoring or just sleeping comfortably; he wondered how they could sleep so easily after what they had done that day.

Nick was afraid to go back to sleep, afraid that he would see the eyes of the dead infant who he had murdered again. He was terrified that his dreams would be filled with the screaming of the infant or the sound of the Jewish man saying his last prayers.

Nick walked out of the room where the others slept, and he found himself outside. He sat with his back against a tree, and deeply inhaled the fresh air, as his mind began to wander. *I was totally convinced that the Nazis' ideas were what we Germans needed, but that was before I witnessed this terrible massacre. I don't know how I can live with myself for taking part in it. I don't know if God was watching, but if he was, he will never forgive me. I will never be able to absolve my conscience for the murders I committed. If Hitler could sanction something like this mass murder, then I was wrong about him. He is not good for Germany or for the German people. I can no longer follow him.*

The killing began again early the following morning. Nick was not sure whether he could actually smell the blood, the fear, and the death, or if he had just imagined a foul odor surrounding them.

"Come on, Wagner," the officer said, rousing Nick from his restless sleep. "Get up and get to work. You made a fool of yourself yesterday but today you can start anew. Let's go."

This time Nick stared at him and shook his head. "No," he said. "I can't do that again today."

"You can, you must, and you will."

Nick continued shaking his head. The officer pulled Nick out of his bunk and tossed him to the floor. "Stand up, Wagner, or I am going to shoot you."

Nick stood up.

"Now, put your shirt on and stop acting like a fool."

Nick put his shirt on.

The officer put a gun in Nick's hand and said, "Let's go." He pushed Nick outside to the ravine where a group of Jews was about to be shot. With his gun pointed at Nick's head, he forced Nick to stand behind a young woman. "Shoot her or I will shoot you," the officer said.

Nick fell to his knees and began to cry. "I am sick from all this killing. Kill me if you must, but I can't do it. I won't do it. I have had enough."

The officer continued pointing his gun at Nick's head. "You stupid fool! Don't make me kill you as an example for the other men."

At that moment, a tall, heavy-set guard rushed over and whispered something to the officer who was about to shoot Nick.

The officer reluctantly lowered his gun away from Nick's head. "Yes, Officer Damzog," he said and walked away.

"Get up," Officer Damzog said to Nick. "Follow me."

Nick did not move. Damzog grabbed Nick by the shoulder and lifted him with one hand. He called over another guard, gestured towards Nick, and said, "Take him."

The other guard grabbed Nick's arm and forced him to follow him to an area where several officers were sitting on folding chairs; some of them were smoking and others were drinking beer. They were talking and laughing as if they were oblivious to the horrors around them. As they approached the group, the guard threw Nick to the ground in front of a tall, handsome officer who was lighting a cigarette. "*Oberstrumführer*," he said.

The *oberstrumführer* puffed on his cigarette then looked at Nick slowly. "What is this about?"

"This young man refuses to participate in the cleansing ritual," the guard said.

"Hmmm, I see. So, why have you brought him here to me? Do you not know how traitors are dealt with?"

"Yes, *Oberstrumführer*." The guard who had brought Nick over to the group of officers was clearly nervous. "However, I wasn't sure what to do because this is Nick Wagner. He is the son of Friedrich Wagner. From what I understand, not only is his father a very good friend of yours, but he has also made large donations to the Nazi Party."

"That's correct," the *oberstrumführer* said, shaking his head and looking at Nick more closely. "It was good that you caught this situation before one of the other guards made an example of this young man. You did well. Now go and leave us."

"Yes, *Oberstrumführer*."

Nick stood in front of the handsome *oberstrumführer*. He was trembling all over, but he stared directly into the other man's eyes.

"So, what happened over there?" the *oberstrumführer* asked.

"I can't do this. I'm sorry. I just can't. War is one thing, but I can't shoot women and babies."

There was a long silence. The *oberstrumführer* took a long drag of his cigarette. He inhaled and then exhaled slowly. Finally, he said, "If it weren't for your father, I would have you shot and thrown into the ravine with the Jews. When you disobey orders, you become an enemy of our Reich. I'm sure you know this. However, since your father is a friend of mine, as a courtesy to him, I'm going to send you home."

Nick's head dropped a little in relief.

"I'm sure you feel like you've won some sort of challenge here today. But believe me, you have done little more than make your father ashamed of you. You are returning not as a hero, but as a weakling," the *oberstrumführer* said, his voice filled with contempt. "I know your father very well and he will not be proud to have such a weak son. I know I wouldn't be pleased if you were my boy. I would probably be doing him a favor if I killed you and put you out of your misery. However, I'm not going to do that. Instead, I'm going to send you back to him and put this situation in his hands. You will be on your way home this afternoon."

As Nick rode away from the ravine in the back of an open-air truck a few hours later, he could not bear to look at the people who stood waiting in line for their turn to die. He turned his face away. *Soon I'll be at the train station and on my way home. Every mile will carry me further away from this hell*, he thought.

FORTY-SIX
1941

A week later, when Nick arrived home, his mother was sitting in the living room knitting. Gloria jumped to her feet when she saw her son; she ran over and hugged him tightly. But when she finally released him, Nick saw the growing sense of horror on her face as she took in his disheveled clothes and the gray, puffy circles surrounding his eyes.

"Are you ill?" Gloria asked in a frightened voice.

"No." Nick shook his head, trying to keep his voice steady so as not to worry her. "I'm alright, Mother."

"I'm so glad you're here, but why have you come home early? I thought you were on a special mission," Gloria said.

"I need to speak to Father. Is he home?" he said, avoiding her question.

"No, he's not. I expect him back later this afternoon. Can I have the maid prepare something for you to eat?"

"Yes, please," Nick said, but his lips were quivering with the effort of trying to smile.

"Gerta," Gloria called out to the maid who had been working for the family for several years. "Can you please fix something for Nick to eat? He's just arrived home after a long journey and he's hungry."

"Yes, of course," Gerta said. She was old enough to be Nick's grandmother.

As Nick watched her go into the kitchen, he felt sorry for her. *At her age she shouldn't have to clean and cook for someone else's family. Why did I never notice this before?* he thought.

"Thank you," Nick said sincerely as Gerta put a plate of stew down in front of him.

Gerta smiled and Nick saw that she was missing several teeth. *Hitler promised that he was going to be good for the German people, but I can see that he hasn't kept that promise,* Nick thought, staring at Gerta and her heartbreaking smile. *Hitler promised to take care of the good German people. He promised them healthcare and arbeit und brot—"work and bread"—to make their lives better.* He recalled how Hitler had taken money from hardworking Germans when he first came to power and put it into accounts for them to purchase automobiles. *But now that he's secure in his position, Hitler is spending that money on this war he is waging with the world,* Nick realized. *That horrible mass murder at Babi Yar has opened my eyes. I can see our Führer in a new light, and frankly, I don't like what I see.*

FORTY-SEVEN

Gloria wore an ice-blue dress as she sat at the dinner table making casual and light conversation with Nick and Friedrich. It was obvious to Nick that his mother was very happy to have him at home. Right now, his father seemed quite happy to see him as well.

However, he couldn't help but worry about how Friedrich was going to react when he heard that Nick had refused to follow orders. Nick wanted to be truthful with his stepfather. He wanted to release the anger that was consuming him. But he was also scared of Friedrich, and he was so nervous that he could hardly eat. Fredrich would be angry that even with all Nick's training to be a good Nazi, he had failed when confronted with a task. *Yet, what does it even mean to be a good Nazi?* Nick wondered. *If it means killing defenseless women and children just because they are Jews, I want no part of it.*

Finally, the meal ended, and Friedrich stood up and excused himself and Nick. "We're going into the study to discuss some important business," Friedrich said to Gloria, who looked at Nick with concern in her eyes.

"What is it, Nick? Is something wrong?" she asked anxiously.

"No, Mother, I'm fine. I promise you. I just need a few minutes to ask Father some questions. Political things. You would find them boring." Nick forced a smile.

Gloria returned his smile, but her lips were trembling. "Alright, but I want you to know that I'm here to listen if you have anything you want to talk to me about," she said gently.

"I know that." Nick walked over and kissed his mother on the top of her head before following Friedrich to the study.

"Sit down, son," Friedrich said as he closed the door.

Nick did as he was told. Friedrich sat down behind his desk and lit a pipe. He took a bottle of schnapps out of his desk drawer and poured two glasses. He handed one to Nick.

"When did you start smoking a pipe?" Nick asked curiously.

"Over the last year or so. I'm getting older." Friedrich sighed. "I find it helps with digestion."

Nick nodded. He could feel his heart racing.

"Now," Friedrich said, taking a sip of schnapps. "What's on your mind, son?"

"I... I..." Nick began. "I don't know how to tell you this because I know that once you hear it, you will be very disappointed in me."

"No need to go on about how I might feel. Just say what you have to say," Friedrich said, leaning in towards him.

Nick cleared his throat. "I was stationed on a job at a ravine in Ukraine. At a place called Babi Yar."

Friedrich nodded but remained silent.

Trembling with suppressed anger and emotion, Nick told his stepfather everything that had happened.

Once Nick had finished speaking, Friedrich sighed. "Sounds like a rather nasty business," he said. "I can see why you didn't want to be a part of it. However, an order is an order."

"I know, Father. I tried to cooperate. I never wanted to cause you shame or disappointment. But I couldn't do it. It was so terrible. Now I feel disillusioned about the Führer and the future of our Fatherland in his hands."

"I realize the Führer has been rather aggressive in his attempts to remove the bad elements who are destructive to our Reich, and I am quite sure that carrying out this order was unpleasant," Friedrich said. He took a large swig of schnapps and emptied his glass, then immediately poured another. "However, if Germany is to rise to its full potential, we must rid ourselves of these *untermenschen*. They are holding us back."

Nick folded his arms over his chest. "I'm sorry, Father, but I can't go back there. I love you and I would try to do anything to please you, but I'm begging you not to send me back. I promise you that I'm not a weak man. I can do what must be done in most situations. However, only if I believe that what I am doing is right. This was not right. I felt it in my soul." Nick began to pace up and down. "Can you imagine how it felt to shoot an infant? Father, it was horrific to look into that ravine and see mounds upon mounds of dead bodies. I've never seen anything as hideous. There were dead women holding their dying children. It was..." He looked away.

Friedrich nodded. "I see," he said, emptying and refilling his glass of schnapps again. "Well, if you can't do it, then you can't. I won't say that I'm not disappointed in you, Nick. I thought you were stronger than that. You are not my son by blood, that's true. However, I raised you and I feel as if you are my own." He shook his head and downed the glass of schnapps. "Important people in the party are going to judge you harshly for avoiding your duty. However, I feel that I must help you. It is not good for our family name for you to be considered an outcast, even a traitor. Therefore, it is essential that you continue working for the good of our Fatherland. That means I must find you a job that will be considered acceptable by the party. Something that assures everyone that you are still a loyal party member. Do you understand me?"

"I do, Father," Nick said quietly. "I truly am sorry for disappointing you."

"Yes, well, I know you didn't do it on purpose," Friedrich said, but Nick could see the disappointment in his father's eyes. "Tomorrow, I'll go into the city and visit some friends of mine. I'll see if I can cash in some favors. Perhaps one of my friends will be able to come up with a job for you that doesn't involve such intense and difficult work."

"You're not angry with me, Father?" Nick asked.

Friedrich shrugged. "I won't lie to you, I feel a bit let down. I don't like to hear that you've failed at anything. After all, you are my son. When I adopted you, you became a Wagner. This means that your behavior reflects on our family. However, I don't know if I could do that job at the ravine. It does sound like messy business. So, I will do what I can to find you cleaner, easier work."

"You don't know how much this means to me," Nick said. "Your opinion of me has always meant the world to me and I never wanted to let you down."

"I know," Friedrich said. "That's why I am going to do what I can to help you."

As the sun beat down on Paris, the hatred in the city intensified. Just last month, like every other Jew in Paris, Chloe had been forced to sew a yellow Star of David on to her clothing. There were strict curfews and Jews had to carry their papers around with them everywhere they went, with a big stamp saying *"Juive"* or *"Jew"* across the page to show they were unable to go unnoticed anymore. The Nazis were lurking around every corner ready to pounce; they would torture a Jewish person for no reason, the way a cat toys with a mouse before killing its prey.

Chloe did everything she could to keep things the same at the dance studio after Maurice's death, but with the recent Aryanization of Jewish businesses, she felt increasingly anxious about losing it. The hardest part was that the studio was not the same without Maurice. She missed him terribly. She missed his constant encouragement, his infectious laughter, and his warm understanding. Even though she was the owner of the studio now, she didn't feel the same joy about her work.

Mimi began working with Chloe. She didn't have the same skills as her grandmother, but she was a good teacher for the young students beginning to study dance. So the classes continued and, as always, to an audience of excited and proud parents, the recitals went on.

After the wedding, Mimi had not felt ready to leave Chloe alone, so they had decided that Michael would move in with them. Chloe and Mimi finished their workday an hour before Michael returned home from university. Therefore, the late afternoons were hectic. Most days Mimi rushed home from the dance studio to start supper; every day except Mondays, which were reserved for weekly trips to the market. Food was being rationed extremely strictly for Jews, and they barely had enough.

Each Monday morning, Mimi and Chloe would wake up early and head to the Jewish market together to purchase enough vegetables, rice, and potatoes for the rest of the week. As they did not have classes on Sunday afternoons, Chloe often went to the general store then to buy enough flour to bake bread for the week. After Maurice's death, all the students paid Chloe directly for their classes, and while she had additional responsibilities with paying the rent and bills for the studio as well as her apartment, it also meant that Chloe was bringing in more money for her family. They used this extra money to buy meat on the black market whenever possible. For her granddaughter's sake, Chloe did her best to make sure they observed the Sabbath each week.

Chloe was happy to watch the newlyweds. She could see that Michael and Mimi were very much in love. They spent every available minute together and, on the weekends, when Michael did not have to go to university, they stayed in bed until early afternoon.

Two years passed, and although the young couple seemed to be attracted to each other like magnets, Mimi did not become pregnant. Chloe never asked Mimi if they were trying or if she was just unable to conceive, but she hoped that they had chosen not to have children because they were waiting for Michael to finish school.

On an exceptionally warm Thursday afternoon, Mimi dismissed her class early. It was too brutally hot to expect little girls to dance.

They were trying to cooperate, but their faces were red and their uniforms were wet with sweat, so she decided to let them go home.

"It's just too hot for the girls today," Mimi said to Chloe, using a towel to wipe sweat from her face. "I'm going to go home and begin preparing dinner."

"I agree," Chloe said. "I know the girls love dancing, but today is just unbearable. I have some work to finish here, but I should be heading home in less than half an hour. Do you have your papers?" she asked. "They've been stopping so many people lately."

"Yes, I know. My papers are right here." Mimi pulled them from her handbag to show Chloe.

"Please be safe, my darling."

"Of course. I'll go straight home."

Mimi washed her face, combed her hair, and left the studio. She walked home quickly. It was nice to have a little extra time to prepare the evening meal. She always felt so rushed.

Back at the apartment, Mimi heard sirens as she began chopping onions and cabbage for dinner. She looked out the window of her apartment and saw several French police trucks pull up on the street outside her building. Mimi peered into the hallway of the building, watching fearfully as the uniformed officers knocked on every door.

At each door they brought out Mimi's Jewish neighbors. Mimi rushed to the window to see a steady stream of her neighbors being forced on to the street. Officers lined them up and loaded them on to trucks.

Then they knocked on Mimi's door. Several sharp knocks. Frozen to the spot in terror, she didn't answer. She heard raised voices outside and footsteps hurrying away. By some miracle the officers must have been distracted by something else. Her heart was racing as she hid behind the curtains, glancing out of the window. She noticed her grandmother walking up the street towards the apartment. *Everything will be alright. There's an explanation for all of this*, Mimi thought, trying to reassure herself.

She suddenly saw two policemen grab Chloe's arms and push her into one of the trucks. Mimi's mouth flew open and although Chloe couldn't hear her, she cried out in horror, *"Bubbie!"*

Mimi ran out of the apartment as fast as she could and approached the police officers who had seized her grandmother. She recognized them both. In fact, she often greeted them when she did her weekly shopping.

"Please," she said, grabbing one of the officers by the sleeve of his uniform. "Tell me what is going on here? Why did you take my grandmother?"

"Go home, hurry up, and lock the door," Chloe yelled out to Mimi from a crowded truck, but her cries came too late. The officer grabbed Mimi and tossed her on to the back of one of the other trucks. She locked eyes with her grandmother for a split second. *I love you so much*, Mimi thought. *What's happening to us?*

The truck rolled through the streets and the police continued to round up all the Jews who lived in the neighborhood. Men, women, children, and infants.

Mimi's heart was slamming in her chest. She wished that she and her *bubbie* were together. Things might be bad, but at least she might not feel so terrified if she could talk to her *bubbie. What about Michael? Was he safe?* He would be terrified if he knew they had been taken in this way.

Once all the trucks were loaded beyond capacity and there was barely enough room to stand, the fleet began to roll in a single-file line.

"Where are they taking us?" a woman with a religious head covering asked, her voice shaking.

"Who knows?" an old man answered fearfully.

The truck was filling with women, children, and old men. There were very few young men among them. Mimi thought of Michael and began to cry.

"The men who came for us are not Germans, they are French

like us. They are the French police. I know so many of them," a young woman said as she gently rocked her baby in her arms.

"They might be French, but they're not like us. They're not Jews," the old man said solemnly.

"But they aren't Nazis. I know them, I tell you. I went to school with one of them," the young woman said. "I don't understand what's happening here."

"My guess is that this whole thing was orchestrated by the Nazis," someone else said.

"But why? Why have they taken us from our homes? What are they planning to do with us?" a woman asked. Her two young children clung tightly to her legs.

"I think they'll probably just question us. I don't think they'll hurt us. They want to show the Germans that they're willing to help make our lives a little more difficult. I don't think we need to worry. After all, these are our French police," another woman said, but her face was etched with anxiety.

The truck hit a bump in the road and the baby awoke with a plaintive cry. The child's mother began singing a lullaby, her voice gentle and soothing. Mimi was suddenly transported back in time, remembering her own mother singing to her. She could barely contain the sob that escaped her chest at the memory.

"I'm scared," a little boy no older than six cried. "My mother isn't here with me. The police took me when I was on my way home from the playground. I don't know where my family are. I want to go home."

"It will be alright. We'll all be back home by nightfall. You'll see." The young mother gave the little boy a smile.

Several of the trucks stopped. The policemen started yelling at the passengers, "Get off the truck and line up."

Mimi did as they asked, but all she could do was search frantically for her grandmother and Michael. There were so many people that she couldn't find them.

A public bus arrived, its engine coughing black smoke into the gray skies. Mimi's legs nearly gave out as a rifle barrel pressed against her spine, pushing her toward the open door of the bus. Around her, neighbors she had known for years stumbled forward —Mrs. Goldstein clutching her prayer book, young Sarah from the bakery sobbing silently with her yellow star already torn and hanging by a thread.

"Move! Move!" The policeman's voice cracked like a whip, but Mimi saw the tremor in his hands as he gripped his weapon.

"Where are we going?" an old man asked him, his hands shaking.

The policeman standing guard wouldn't meet his eyes. He turned his head sharply away and gave the old man another rough shove. "Don't ask questions."

Mimi's heart hammered against her ribs as the terrible understanding crashed over her: this was what they had all whispered about in the shadows. *This was the end.* The bus door slammed shut with a metallic clang that sounded like a prison gate closing forever.

FORTY-NINE

The convoy of trucks and buses stopped in front of the Vélodrome d'Hiver, an indoor sportsplex. As each truck was emptied, the passengers were escorted at gunpoint into the large building. Mimi searched frantically for her grandmother and her husband, pushing her way through the crowds. But there were hordes of people, and it was impossible to find her family.

She recognized several of her neighbors, but when she asked if they had seen Michael or Chloe, no one had. Night fell like a dark shroud. The sound of weeping could be heard throughout the huge space. Mimi waited nervously, hoping to be released soon, but no one came to release her or to explain why she was being detained in this large facility. No food or water had been provided and by morning everyone was hungry.

The bathroom facilities were already broken. A strong odor of sweat, feces, urine, and vomit permeated the air. Mimi sank down in a corner on the cold concrete floor and buried her head in her hands. Her bladder felt as if it might explode, but the stench coming from the toilets made her sick to her stomach. *I have to go, so I must do this,* she thought as she entered the bathroom where the smell was even stronger. Gagging, she quickly urinated and ran out. Her nose was running and her eyes were wet with tears. She was exhausted, but fear of what might come next left her unable to rest.

She leaned her head against the wall. *Bubbie, where are you? Michael, are you here?*

Mimi lost count of how many days had passed. She only knew that the sun had risen and set several times, and still no food or water had been provided. Now, the bathroom facilities were overflowing with human waste. Just a few feet away from her, she saw the young mother who had ridden in the truck with her. The woman was weeping. In her arms she held the remains of her child. The baby was dead. Mimi could not bear to look.

Then, one morning, the police began to load the prisoners back on to the trucks. As the crowd moved forward, Mimi's eyes scanned the groups of prisoners in search of her family, but once again she couldn't find them. She was alone.

This time, children were separated from their parents and sent away. Adults were forced to go in another direction. Mothers screamed and wept. They begged the French police to let their children go with them, but the police paid them no attention. Soon they were on their way.

On this journey, no one spoke. The only sound that could be heard in the back of the truck was people quietly weeping.

The following morning, the convoy of trucks stopped in front of a freight train. Some of the prisoners were stuffed into boxcars. Mimi was in line to board and enter one of the boxcars, but the young French police officer who had been loading them into the train put up his hand. "This one is full," he said to the man who seemed to be in charge of the French national police.

"All of the boxcars are stuffed. The entire train is full. Put the rest of them back on the truck. We'll take them to Drancy until the next train arrives," he replied.

Drancy? Where and what is Drancy? Mimi thought, consumed by panic. *How am I ever going to get home to Bubbie and Michael? Bubbie, help me! Please help me! Where are you? Where have they taken you?*

A flash of terror rose in Mimi that was so strong that she forgot to control herself. She grabbed the sleeve of the policeman's uniform. "Please, please, officer, I'm begging you. Let me get on that train. I think my *Bubbie* is on that train and I must go wherever she is going. Please, I'm small and slender, just push me in. I don't care how uncomfortable I am."

"*Bubbie?* What's a *bubbie?* I don't know that word, but it sounds like a Jew word to me," he said, laughing.

"My grandmother," Mimi said, tugging on his sleeve as tears began to roll down her cheeks. "Please, I cannot be separated from her. I must get on that train."

"How dare you touch my uniform with your filthy Jew hand! Get in the truck before I make you sorry," the policeman warned. He was annoyed now and no longer laughing.

Mimi was frozen. She couldn't move as she watched the train spring to life. "No, no, please don't go without me."

The policeman slapped her hard across the face, splitting her lip.

Mimi staggered back, her ears ringing as blood ran down her chin. *I must be strong, I must be strong.* "I think my husband and my grandmother are on that train. I'm begging you to take pity on me. My family has been separated. Please tell me how I can get to my family. I'm begging you! I will give you anything you want. I have money at home. I promise you that I'll pay you whatever I have as soon as I get there."

But the policeman was no longer paying attention to her. Another officer, who was several years older, approached her. "Do what he says," the older policeman whispered in her ear, his eyes kind as he helped her on to the truck. "He's in charge, and he's not going to listen to anything you have to say. Here, take this," he said, handing her his handkerchief. "Your lip is bleeding."

Mimi took the handkerchief. Making one last attempt she asked, "Can you help me? Please? I'll pay you whatever you ask as soon as I get home. Can you find my grandmother and my husband and send us home?"

The older officer shook his head. "I'm sorry," he said and walked away.

Another guard kept watch over the truck, his gun constantly pointed at the prisoners. By the time the truck began to move, it had become part of a convoy of trucks overloaded with women and children. Mimi stood numbly, dabbing at the blood from her lip with the handkerchief.

It was not long before the convoy arrived at a large complex where the prisoners were forced to exit the trucks. Some of the prisoners had managed to hold on to their children when the police tried to take them earlier, but once they were inside the complex, the children were separated from their parents. They were screaming and crying.

When the officers demanded that the mothers send their children away with a group of officers, one of the mothers refused to release her young son. The boy seemed to be about five or six years old. He was a small, skinny child with a bright-red rash on his face. Mimi felt sorry for him, but the police officer did not. He was overwhelmed by the responsibilities of trying to control so many prisoners. Not knowing what else to do, the guard tried to pull the child away from his mother, but she held him tightly. Everyone was watching, and Mimi could see that the officer was getting angry. His face was scarlet, and he stopped trying to pull the boy away. He stood looking at the mother who stared back at him in defiance. His eyes were narrowed and his fists were clenched. This woman was making him look weak and foolish and he was livid. He said, "You have one minute to give me the boy or I'm going to be forced to take action."

The mother shook her head. She buried her face in her son's neck. "No, no, I will not give him to you," she said, shaking. The child, sensing his mother's fear, began to cry. All eyes were on the officer. Mimi could see that he wasn't going to back down. She held her breath as he raised his gun.

"No," Mimi whispered under her breath. "No."

If the policeman heard Mimi, he ignored her. There was no sign of mercy in his face. He shot the child first. The child died instantly. A guttural scream erupted from his mother's lips.

A smile that said, "*I won. I have power over all of you, so you had better listen to me,*" came over the officer's face.

He gave the mother a moment to grieve. Not out of pity, but because he was enjoying his victory. Then he shot her, too. For a moment, there was silence as all the prisoners stared in horror.

The officer broke the silence. "Let this be a lesson to you," he said loudly and proudly, "when an officer of the law tells you to do something, you don't question it. You do as you're told." He glared at them. "Now, get into the line over there," he said, indicating a group that was primarily of women of working age as well as a few old men. There were no children in that line. To the right, another line had formed of little children. They were being led away as if by a pied piper. Somehow, Mimi felt sure that they would never be seen again.

For a long time, the prisoners stood in line with the hot sun blazing down on their shoulders. They were warned not to speak to each other. After watching the officer murder the mother and child —their dead bodies still lay in a pool of blood just a few feet away— no one dared to defy the policemen.

FIFTY

A German officer, annoyed by the heat, removed his hat and pushed his hair away from his face. He replaced his hat and sauntered over to the group of prisoners.

Turning to the French policeman, he said in an authoritative voice, "I need three girls as soon as possible. Nice-looking girls are preferable. By that I mean, get ones that have some Aryan features —blonde hair, blue eyes. Do you understand?"

Mimi had been half-listening to the officer and policeman's conversation, but she had been distracted by seeing someone who she thought she recognized among the group of prisoners. It was a man she had always admired, a famous Jewish choreographer who she had met once at a gala that Maurice had given. His name was Rene Blum and although he was not handsome, she remembered him being very refined and well-dressed. She recalled Rene's pleasant demeanor and easy smile. Mimi had been in awe of him when they met and she had hardly been able to speak, but he was not the same now. His clothes were dirty and torn; he was hunched over and painfully thin. She was glad that Rene didn't see her because she wouldn't have known what to say to him in this place.

"You," the German officer said in a firm voice as he pointed to

Mimi, jolting her from her memories of happier times. "Follow me."

Mimi jumped when she saw the officer single her out. For a moment she didn't move. She stood paralyzed, her mouth gaping open as she stared at him in fear and disbelief. *What does he want with me?*

"I said, follow me," he repeated sternly. Then his voice suddenly changed and became less threatening, almost soft, "Don't be afraid. It's your lucky day."

But Mimi was afraid, she was terrified. She didn't trust him. This could be a terrible trick. She had heard that the Nazis would do things that were purposely cruel just to see how their victims would react. But as he led her and two other young blonde women away from the rest of the group, even though her knees were weak and her legs were trembling, she couldn't help but hope that she might be going home. *Is it possible that I'm going to be freed?* she wondered. *Maybe the officer will turn out to be a good person. I'll try to find an opportunity to ask him where they've taken Bubbie and Michael.*

The three young women were ushered into the back seat of a black automobile. Mimi glanced over at her two companions. They were quiet, but she could see the fear in their eyes. The Nazi officer climbed into the front seat beside the driver who had been waiting for his return. The driver turned the key and the auto sprang into life.

Mimi felt her heart race. *We're on our way somewhere, but where?*

One of the young women began scratching her arms nervously. Mimi couldn't bear to watch her as she was drawing blood. The girl's arm was red, and an angry rash had appeared. Mimi reached over and took the girl's hand in hers. "We'll be alright," she whispered.

"How do you know?"

"I just know," Mimi lied.

No one spoke as the car sped through the city with the three young women huddled together in the back seat. Each of them was blonde and blue-eyed. They gave the appearance of being Aryan which Mimi knew that the Germans found more appealing than dark hair and eyes. This made her worry that the three of them might have been chosen to be sent to some sort of brothel. The idea sent a chill through her, but she dared not ask any questions.

When the car pulled up in front of Levitan, the previously Jewish-owned department store in Paris where Maurice had purchased furniture for the studio as she and Rose fantasized about their futures, Mimi glanced at the two girls on either side of her. *What are we doing here?* she thought. One of the girls shook her head and shrugged as if she could read Mimi's mind.

"Follow me," the Nazi said as the driver opened the door to the automobile so the girls could get out.

The girl beside Mimi who had been scratching herself began to cry. Mimi squeezed her hand. "You'll be alright. Come on now. Don't cry. I'm here with you."

The Nazis led the girls inside the building where they found that a new shop had been set up. It was no longer a posh furniture palace belonging to Wolf Levitan; it was now a department store owned and operated by the Nazi Party.

As they walked through the store, Mimi saw that all the employees wore striped uniforms and numbered armbands. Some of them were standing at counters waiting on customers. The customers ranged from regular people dressed in civilian clothes to Nazis in uniform. In one of the rooms, a group of prisoners was busy sorting through the contents of large wooden crates, separating housewares, furs, and clothing into separate piles.

"Heil Hitler!" The Nazi saluted one of the officers who seemed to be in charge of the workers.

"Heil Hitler!"

The Germans were friendly and looked to know each other. "I brought these three females from Drancy, Fritz."

"Would you look at that one? Just take a look at her hair. It's so blonde it's almost white. Must have Aryan blood somewhere."

"I think all three of them do. I actually chose these three because I thought it would be a shame to shave their hair off, and I know you don't do that here at the store."

"I quite agree with you. If the German *hausfrauen* come shopping, they'll certainly feel more at ease if the salesgirls have hair on their heads." He laughed. "It makes it seem more like a regular shop."

"Exactly."

"I'll take them from here. I have a woman who'll train them on what they need to do to work here."

"Good. I'll be on my way then."

"Let's have dinner at my house one night next week. I'll ask Alice to call your wife and arrange it."

"I look forward to it."

The three women stood quietly, trying not to draw attention to themselves.

After the officer who brought them left, a woman dressed in a uniform different from the striped uniform the prisoners wore was called over to the group. She was slender and although her uniform was clean and pressed, she was not pretty or professional looking.

Her dirty blonde hair was greasy and pulled severely into a tight knot at the back of her neck. "Elke. These three prisoners are new. They were just brought over from Drancy. Explain our operation to them and show them the rooms on the top floor where they will be sleeping."

Elke nodded and turned to the new recruits. "Follow me," she said coldly. She spoke French, but her accent was distinctly German. "Everything you see here is for sale. It's all secondhand. However, most of it is good quality."

Mimi, still holding the trembling hand of the girl who had been scratching herself, followed behind. There were several floors in the building. One had furniture, some of it plain but some pieces very expensive and ornate. The next floor held pots and pans of all shapes and sizes as well as kitchen utensils.

Mimi saw a young German woman with curly blonde hair

standing at the counter talking to a Jewish salesclerk with a numbered armband. The German woman was purchasing a large, heavy soup pot and for a moment Mimi stared at the pot and wondered where it had come from. *Is it possible that all these things were stolen from the homes of arrested Jews? Could that pot have once been used by a bubbie to make chicken soup for her family?* These thoughts passed through Mimi's mind, and they made her sick with worry for the safety of her own grandmother.

As the three new recruits followed the Nazi called Elke, they passed a group of women seated at sewing machines. The sound of the machines was almost deafening. Mimi watched them, with their heads bowed over their work. "Many of our customers require alterations so we need seamstresses. Can any of you sew?" Elke asked the three girls.

For a moment none of them answered. Mimi considered the situation. *At least if I am useful to the Nazis, I won't get transferred to a place that might be worse than this,* she thought. *I'd rather sew than be used in a brothel.*

"Yes, I can sew," Mimi blurted out. Her grandmother had taught her to sew because they had often needed to alter costumes for dance recitals.

"Good, then you can work here with these ladies. You'll be making alterations for customers, and you'll also be required to fix any goods that come in that need repairing. The better you are at your job, the lighter your workload will be. I suggest you make every piece you touch look new."

The girl holding Mimi's hand squeezed it hard. Then she said, "I can sew, too. My mother was a seamstress. She taught me to sew. I can make wedding gowns."

"Then you'll work here in the sewing room as well."

Well, at least we will be together, Mimi thought.

FIFTY-ONE

Over the next few months Mimi learned that the name of the girl she had befriended was Gisele. She also learned that Gisele had lied so she could work with Mimi. Gisele had no experience as a seamstress.

On that first night when they collapsed with exhaustion on to their mattresses on the top floor of the building, Gisele explained that she was terrified to be without Mimi. "I realize that we've just met, but you're the only person I know here." She was trying to hold back her tears as she spoke. "I feel so lost and so alone. I don't know where they've taken my family. In fact, I can't say whether they are alive or not. So, please, I know it's a lot to ask, but can you be my sister? You have no one here either."

"Of course I'll be your sister," Mimi replied gently. She was glad to have a friend who she could lean on. And she taught Gisele to sew.

In the beginning, the work seemed endless and very difficult. Gisele, not knowing anything about sewing, struggled to complete her tasks. Sometimes, even though Mimi had more than enough work of her own, she would take a few pieces from Gisele's pile and work on them. Whenever the guards were busy talking among themselves, Mimi taught Gisele a little more. Since Gisele was young and smart, and she knew her life depended upon learning this trade, she picked it up quickly.

Every day, crates of new merchandise arrived. They went to the special sorting area to be processed. Depending on the condition of the goods, some of the things were immediately displayed in the showroom, some of the clothing was sent up to the sewing floor for repair, and some pieces of furniture were sent to another floor to be restored. Other pieces were boxed and shipped out. The store's hours of operation were long, but they did not end when the store closed. Once the shop was shut to the public, the prisoners were responsible for cleaning down their work areas.

Mimi managed to endure the long days at her sewing machine. At night, when she was upstairs getting ready to go to sleep or when she was eating her meal, she met several other prisoners who had come from camps such as Auschwitz-Birkenau. When they told Mimi of the terrible things that went on in those places, she realized that this job working at the department store had saved her life. She tried not to think about her *bubbie* or her husband. It was too painful. Instead, she forced herself to focus on each task at hand until it was done.

Four months later, the head of the sewing department told the seamstresses that they were expecting a visit from three top Nazi officials and therefore the store must be cleaned from top to bottom. The store was to remain open to customers the day before the arrival of the guests, but the prisoners would be required to do all the cleaning after closing. No one would be permitted to sleep the night before the visit.

"I'm so tired," Gisele said. "I'm afraid I'm going to fall asleep at the sewing machine."

"I know you're exhausted. I'm tired, too, but you must not fall asleep. If you do, they'll punish you harshly for embarrassing them in front of these top Nazis. Stay awake, Gisele. You must."

. . .

At about ten o'clock in the morning a few days after their briefing by the head of the sewing department, three well-fed and well-dressed Nazi officials came walking slowly through each floor of the shop. They inspected everything and made several demands of the guards. When they got to the sewing floor, Mimi glanced up at them for a moment and then turned her attention back to her work. Her heart was pounding so hard that it felt like thunder in her ears. Gisele stole a glance at Mimi. Mimi nodded at Gisele and motioned to her to pay attention to her work.

One of the Nazi officers stopped in front of Mimi and watched her for a moment. Mimi forced herself to keep her head down, but her hands were trembling so badly that she was afraid she was going to lose control of her sewing machine. Ever so gently, the Nazi put his hand under Mimi's chin and forced her to lift her face so he could see her better.

"What is this one doing here in the sewing room? A girl who looks so Aryan should not be hiding up here in the sewing room. She would be better for business working on the sales floor. Move her immediately. I want her where the shoppers can see her."

Until this moment, Mimi had been grateful that they had not shaved her head. Some of the other prisoners talked about how lucky they were to be working at this store because they were permitted to keep their hair. But now Mimi realized that this Nazi official had seen her light blonde hair and decided that because of this she should be in the public eye.

Glancing at Gisele, she saw the terror in her eyes. They were going to be separated. Mimi had grown accustomed to working beside her friend each day and it had given them both the strength to continue. Mimi could already feel that this change was going to be hard on them both.

"Stand up, girl," the Nazi official said to Mimi.

Mimi knew better than to argue. She stood up but kept her head and eyes cast down.

"Put her in the section that sells jewelry," he said. "She's actually quite pretty for a Jew, so that should be the perfect place for her."

Gisele was breathing hard, so hard that Mimi could hear her. Mimi knew Gisele well enough to know that she wanted to go with her. She could see that her friend was trying to find the courage to ask permission, but Mimi knew that this would be a mistake. *Don't say a word,* she thought, desperately hoping that Gisele wouldn't risk making a request to the Nazis. *Don't ask them if you can be moved to come with me. These Nazis might seem quiet and easygoing, but they aren't. If you say a word or complain, they'll hurt you. Let's just hope that we'll be able to keep our sleeping arrangements. Don't ask for anything, Gisele. Please just be quiet.*

It was as if Gisele heard Mimi's thoughts because she remained silent. As much as Mimi wanted to look back at her friend, she dared not as she followed a female guard who led her downstairs to another floor where there were lines of beautiful glass display cases filled with all types of jewelry. Necklaces, cuff links, rings, and earrings constructed from shiny gold, silver, and platinum, and filled with sparkling diamonds and brightly colored gems of all sizes and shapes.

"You will work here," the guard said, indicating the cases of jewelry. "There are many beautiful things here, but you had better keep your wits about you and keep your hands off. If you are caught stealing anything, you will not be shot immediately." She gave Mimi a hollow smile that made her shiver. "Or worse, your hands will be chopped off and you will be put outside where you will be left to bleed to death. Do you understand me?"

Mimi nodded. She felt tears welling in her eyes. She understood well enough that these Nazis were heartless.

The guard called one of the prisoners over to her—a middle-aged woman with golden hair and kind green eyes. "You will train this girl to be a saleswoman. Teach her how to examine diamonds and stones," the guard said. "Start now."

"Yes, ma'am."

As the guard walked away, the older woman introduced

herself. "I'm Ruth," she said warmly. She leaned in and whispered, "You look frightened. It's going to be okay."

"I don't know anything about jewels," Mimi replied anxiously.

"It's alright. Don't be afraid. Before I was arrested and brought here, my husband and I owned a jewelry store. He was a diamond cutter, so I know all about the different metals and stones. I'll teach you everything I know."

"I'm Mimi," she said to Ruth. "Thank you in advance for everything."

That night Mimi was pleased to learn that her sleeping arrangements had not changed. When Gisele came upstairs to their room, both women cried and hugged each other. From then on, each night she and Gisele would lie on their mattress and whisper until the lights were turned out.

"I hate working in the sewing room without you," Gisele said one evening.

"I know. I wish we could work together, but we have no choice. We must be grateful that at least we have the evenings together," Mimi said.

Gisele nodded and reached out and grabbed Mimi's hand. She squeezed it tightly and they both sobbed together until they fell asleep.

FIFTY-TWO

AUSCHWITZ, 1943

The train came to an abrupt stop and although the people in the boxcar were packed so tightly that they were unable to move, the entire group was thrown forward. A woman screamed and a small child began to cry. The sound of metal slamming against metal thundered as bright sunlight shot into the boxcar.

Chloe had lost count of how many days she had spent in the darkness of the boxcar with its noxious odors of feces, urine, and vomit. The rays of the sun hurt her eyes, and she reached up to cover them for a moment. But there was no time to adjust to the light. Guards in Nazi uniforms were demanding that the prisoners climb out of the train. "*Mach schnell,*" they yelled as the prisoners rushed out the door. Chloe had once lived in Germany, so she knew that the guards were shouting at them to hurry up.

Once outside, everyone was forced to line up and then a selection process began. As each prisoner reached the front of the line, a man with dark hair and a space between his front teeth either pointed to the left or to the right. The young woman in front of Chloe cried out as she was separated from her mother and her child. They were sent to the left, while the young woman was sent to the right.

Chloe felt her legs almost give way beneath her. *Just keep moving. I must be strong,* she thought.

The man with the dark hair studied Chloe for a moment before pointing to the right. She followed the young woman into another line. Her eyes scanned the crowds frantically in search of her granddaughter. She didn't see her anywhere.

Along with the others in her line, Chloe was herded toward a low concrete building. SS guards barked orders while prisoners in striped uniforms moved efficiently around them, avoiding eye contact. The air was thick with the smell of disinfectant and human fear.

"Remove all clothing. Everything. Quickly!"

Chloe's fingers trembled as she unbuttoned her coat. Around her, people stood naked and shivering—mothers trying to shield children, everyone's eyes vacant with shock.

The cold spray of water hit like needles. Rough hands grabbed her, shoving her under the shower heads where harsh soap stung her eyes.

Then she was sent into a line where a Jewish male prisoner took a dirty needle and wrote a number into the delicate skin of her forearm: 34629, a tattoo that would become her name and follow her for the rest of her life.

"You no longer have names. Memorize the numbers on your arms because this is your identity from now on," a guard said.

Chloe had never had a tattoo. It was against the Jewish religion. Although the prisoner had tried to be gentle, the needle was dirty and it was very painful. Still bleeding, she was ushered into another line. The tattoo had injured her body, but the Nazis were going to attempt to destroy her soul.

When Chloe came to the front of the line she was forced to sit in a chair while a female prisoner shaved her head. Throughout her life she had thought of her hair as her best feature, a symbol of beauty. She remembered how her husband had loved to run his fingers through it. He said it looked like a delicate field of winter wheat. Chloe bit her lip until she tasted blood as she watched her golden locks fall to the ground. *I will not cry. I will not let them see me cry.*

The guard yelled, "Next."

Bleeding and bald, Chloe was handed a uniform, a spoon, and a bowl. Then she, along with a large group of prisoners, was sent to a building that was filled with dirty, stained bunk beds. Their room stank from human waste, sweat, and the lack of fresh air. As there was no space available, the new arrivals clamored for a place to sleep. Each bed was packed with women. Chloe looked around but she could not find an open space. Just as Chloe was beginning to give up on finding anywhere to sleep, a young woman motioned to her. "Over here. There's an opening."

Chloe walked over. "Thank you," she said.

The girl nodded. "Aren't you Chloe Mandel-Levin, the dancer?"

"Yes," Chloe said. "I'm surprised you could recognize me in this state." She reached up and touched her now-bald head.

"I've always admired you," the young woman said.

Chloe blushed.

"I wanted to dance when I was younger, but my parents thought it was a waste of time. They said I didn't have the talent for it. I suppose it would have been a waste. I mean, look where we both ended up," she whispered, her voice breaking.

Chloe had no answers for her. She sat down on the edge of the bed. Her eyes immediately searched the room for Mimi, but she didn't see her anywhere. *Mimi, where are you?* she thought. Chloe would die for Mimi, but how could she protect her now?

Then a kapo, a Jewish woman who had been appointed by the Nazis, began to explain the rules. Roll call was at three thirty in the morning and again in the evening. "You will receive three meals a day. Coffee in the morning," she said.

"If you can call them meals," someone called out.

"Shut your mouth or I'll report you to the guards," the kapo shouted.

The prisoners immediately went silent.

"You'll receive your work detail at the next roll call," she said.

The roll call began when the prisoners arrived back at the camp from their daily jobs, and it was grueling. Chloe was forced to stand at attention for several hours before the guard began to call out the prisoners' numbers. When it was finally over, the prisoners were sent off to their work details. Some were selected for labor at the rubber factory, others were used for construction work.

Chloe, along with another woman, was chosen to supervise and control the incoming children before they were sent off to a special children's camp.

"I'm Ida Rosensweig," the other woman said, introducing herself to Chloe. She had a Star of David sewn on her striped uniform, so Chloe knew she was also Jewish. She appeared to be several years younger than Chloe. Her eyes were the color of coffee, warm and gentle.

"I'm Chloe," Chloe said.

"I know. One of the other girls told me that you were a famous dancer. Is it true?"

"I wouldn't say I was famous," Chloe said modestly, "but I was a ballerina."

"I would have loved to be a famous ballerina."

Chloe laughed. "So would I, but I never got that far. I hurt my ankle in an accident, and I was unable to continue dancing professionally."

"That's such a shame," Ida said.

"I suppose, but I got married and had a family." Chloe sighed. "I'd give anything to be with them again."

"Me too. I miss my sisters."

Chloe nodded sadly. "I miss my granddaughter. I don't know what happened to her."

They fell silent as a guard appeared before them. "You two are responsible for the children when the transports arrive. You must take them away from their parents and keep them quiet until a truck arrives to take them to the children's camp."

Ida nodded, her eyes cast downwards, but Chloe held the guard's gaze.

He slapped her across the face. "Don't you dare look at me! When I talk to you, you look down at the ground. Do you understand?"

Chloe felt her eyes smart and her cheeks sting, but she nodded quickly.

"Good. A transport will be arriving this afternoon. The two of you Jew swine are very lucky because this happens to be one of the better jobs at the camp. So, if I find that either of you can't perform it to my satisfaction, you will be transferred to a job that is far worse than this. Do you understand me?"

"Yes," Chloe and Ida answered in unison.

"Now, since you have some time before the transport arrives and the last group of children shipped out yesterday, you can go and help out in the kitchen."

FIFTY-THREE

The job assignment that Chloe was given was worse than she could have ever imagined. It was heart-wrenching. The children were terrified. They had been ripped from their mothers' arms and then Ida and Chloe were sent to collect them. Their screaming and crying unnerved Chloe. By the end of the day, she was shattered and trembling. The children were so lost and alone that they quickly became attached to Chloe and Ida, making it even more difficult to send them away when the truck arrived to take them.

Although she was exhausted, Chloe found it difficult to sleep. The hot summer air was stifling, and the women were pushed together in their beds like sardines. Lice-infested straw covered the beds and the floor. She woke every morning covered in angry red bites that itched all day. Showers or baths were only permitted once a week, and the slop bucket filled with urine and feces was always overflowing. Each day, the women awoke to find that some of their fellow prisoners had died during the night. It was their responsibility to report the deaths to the guards and then to drag the bodies out of the block and lay them on top of the ever-growing piles of corpses.

Typhoid broke out in the camp and the deaths increased each day to frightening numbers. Women moaned in pain all night, but they still went to work in the morning because anyone who showed any signs of being sick was sent to the hospital and never returned. Before she went to sleep every night, Chloe prayed that if Mimi was anywhere in this manmade hell, she would not come down with the disease.

As the summer turned to autumn, the oppressive heat began to fade and the typhoid epidemic subsided. However, things were only better for a short time. The prisoners who had been at the camp for over a year warned that the winter was coming, and it would be even more brutal than the summer had been.

More transports arrived each day and with them came children, always frightened and hungry. Having no food to give them, Chloe sang to them. With tears in her eyes, she softly purred the lullaby that she had sung to Lily and then to Mimi. It comforted them until the truck arrived to take them away and then panic set in.

"Don't worry so much about them," one of the kapos said. "They're going to be fine. I hear the camp where they are sent is very nice."

"Do you really believe that?" Ida asked.

"Of course, I do," the kapo replied.

Ida shook her head. "I don't know."

Chloe didn't trust the kapo either.

Ruth was only permitted a short amount of time to train Mimi before Mimi was expected to stand behind the counter on the sales floor without any assistance. On the first day that Mimi was alone, a young French girl walked in holding on to the arm of a tall, smiling SS officer.

The girl slowly scanned each of the display cases as she made her way around the room. When she saw Mimi, the girl's eyes lit up. She whispered something to her male companion and walked over to where Mimi stood wearing a uniform with a Star of David on the breast.

"Mimi, do you remember me?" the girl asked.

Mimi studied her. The girl did look familiar, but she couldn't place her. "I'm sorry. You look familiar, but I don't recall your name," she said.

"I'm Astrid. I was one of the dance students. I studied under your wonderful grandmother. She was something. Quite the dancer." The girl smiled. "Ah, that seems like a lifetime ago. In those days I was rather shy. Perhaps that's why you can't remember me, but I still remember you. You were the prettiest little girl I have ever seen. All the girls at the studio said so. You're still very beautiful. I guess you just keep getting prettier as the years pass." Astrid smiled, but her lips were trembling.

"Thank you. You're very kind." Mimi forced a smile, but she looked down at the ground.

"Things certainly didn't work out the way we thought they would, did they?" The French girl glanced at the Star of David on Mimi's uniform and then looked away.

"No, they certainly did not," Mimi replied sadly.

"My mother always tells me that even though things are bad for us, we must be thankful that at least we're not Jewish," Astrid said. "But I can't help but feel bad. I have far too many Jewish friends not to feel very terrible when I think about all that has happened to our Jewish neighbors."

"Yes, well, your mother is probably right. You should be glad that you aren't Jewish. Is that man, the SS officer you're with, your husband?" Mimi asked.

"Oh no, we aren't married. He's just a man who comes to see me occasionally."

"Oh. I see," Mimi said, looking away. She realized that Astrid was probably dating Germans to get extra rations or money for her family and herself. Mimi had heard that a lot of French girls had compromised their principles to survive.

"I always liked your family," Astrid said, "and I liked Maurice, too. He was a nice man. I was shocked and horrified by what happened to him." Her voice trailed off. "I can still remember how kind your grandmother was to me. When my father lost his job and my parents couldn't afford to pay for dance lessons anymore, your grandmother insisted that I continue. She refused to accept any payment. She said the money was not as important to her as fulfilling the dreams of a little girl." Astrid sighed and then she whispered just loud enough for Mimi to hear, "I still get chills when I remember looking out my window and seeing those two Germans murder your husband, his poor sister, and their parents. Oh, Mimi. I was so sorry that happened to you. You and your family didn't deserve such terrible treatment. I wish I could do something to help you, I really do. I wanted to help that day, but I'm ashamed to admit that I was too afraid. I ran away from the window and hid."

Michael, murdered. Mimi could barely process the words as her vision began to blur. She gripped the countertop to steady herself.

"They... They murdered my husband?" Mimi was shaking as she choked out the words.

"You didn't know?" Astrid replied, her eyes full of horror.

"No." Mimi shook her head frantically. "Please tell me everything you know. Please tell me what you saw."

"It was during the roundup. There was chaos in the streets. I heard the commotion outside, so I looked out my window. I saw Rose being attacked by one of the officers. Your father-in-law tried to fight him off, but he was too weak and they pushed him to the ground. That's when your husband stepped in. He was shaking one of the French police officers; he was fighting with the policeman, yelling something. I couldn't hear him, so I don't know what he was saying, but the policeman just shook his head and turned away. Then two Nazi officers walked up. And... well—"

"Go on. Please. I must know what you saw," Mimi said, her gut twisting with fear. "I need to know what happened to my Michael."

"Are you sure you want me to tell you?" Astrid said.

"I'm sure." Mimi's heart was racing. She felt dizzy and sick like she might vomit, but she had to know.

"One of the Nazis hit Michael in the face with his gun. Michael fell to the ground next to his father. The Nazi was shouting in German and then he pointed his gun and shot Michael, Rose, and their parents." Tears began to well in Astrid's eyes. "I am so sorry, Mimi. I am so sorry."

"Are you sure my husband is dead? Perhaps he lived?" Mimi's hands were shaking, but her voice was hopeful.

"He's dead, Mimi. The Nazi shot Michael in the face. I saw

the whole thing." Tears fell down Astrid's cheeks. "I wish I wasn't the one to tell you."

Mimi put her hand on her throat. It felt dry like sandpaper, and she could not speak, but she forced herself to try. She lowered her voice to a whisper, conscious of the SS officer browsing a few meters away, "And my grandmother? Do you know what happened to her?"

Astrid shook her head. "I don't know. I never saw her again after the roundup."

Just then, the SS officer walked back over to Astrid. "Are you crying, my dear? Has this girl done something to offend you?" He looked down at Mimi with pure contempt.

"Oh no, no. I got something in my eye. It's nothing really." Astrid tried to smile at him.

"Well, that's good," the Nazi said. "Now, have you found a trinket that suits your fancy?"

Astrid shook her head.

"No, nothing suits you? Astrid, my dear, that's rather unusual for you, isn't it? I know how much you love pretty things. You've been over here talking for such a long time I thought you were probably undecided." He turned to Mimi and said, "Show her that necklace, the one in the front of the case with the green stone." He pointed to a gold necklace. "Is that an emerald?"

"Yes, it is." Mimi's voice cracked and she cleared her throat. Her hands were trembling as she took the necklace out of the case and handed it to Astrid.

The Nazi helped Astrid to put it on.

"Do you like it?" Astrid asked the Nazi.

"Yes, actually, it's quite pretty," he said. He turned to Mimi. "What do you think?"

"Yes, it's lovely," she said. She knew that she must not show her anger or pain, but all she could think about was Michael. In her mind's eye she saw his smile and remembered the way he looked at her when they stood under the *chuppah*—the canopy—on their wedding day. *Even the memories of that precious night had been ruined by the Nazis' hatred towards us.*

"We'll take that necklace," the Nazi said, bringing Mimi back to the present.

Mimi nodded. She was relieved to be able to walk away from Astrid and her boyfriend so that she could ask one of the German guards to complete the transaction. She wasn't allowed to take money from the customers.

As soon as Astrid and the Nazi left the store, Mimi found Ruth. She pretended to be asking Ruth a question about a piece of jewelry, but really, she was telling her what Astrid had told her about Michael.

Ruth squeezed her hand and said, "I'm so sorry for you. But you can't let yourself dwell on it or you will go out of your mind. There is nothing you can do to change it. You have to do your best to put it behind you and try to look forward. All we can do is pray that better times will come."

That night, Mimi looked desperately for Gisele—she needed to tell her everything that had happened that day with Astrid. She rushed up the stairs to the sleeping quarters and searched anxiously for her friend, but she couldn't see her. Mimi found one of the girls who had worked at the sewing machines with them. "Hannah, have you seen Gisele?" she asked.

"Yes, haven't you heard? It was terrible," Hannah said.

"What was terrible?" Mimi asked.

"Gisele couldn't make her quota, so she was dragged out of the department store and sent away. Everyone thinks she was sent to a camp. Probably killed."

"Dear God," Mimi said, sinking down on to one of the mattresses. "Are you sure?"

"I'm sure they sent her away, but I'm not sure where they sent her. I wouldn't dwell on it. If you do, it will cost you your sanity.

People come and they go. You must not get too attached," Hannah said and then went downstairs to get in line for her evening meal.

Mimi couldn't eat. She lay awake, blaming herself for Gisele's misfortune. All night she wept and vowed to herself that she would not make any more friends. Friendship left her heart open and her soul far too vulnerable.

FIFTY-FIVE

Winter descended quickly, her icy fingers stretched across Poland, strangling the weak and killing even more prisoners as she made her way through the camp.

As Chloe and Ida waited for the daily transport, a tall, well-built man in an SS uniform approached them. "Chloe?" he said.

Hearing her name, Chloe whirled around. She recognized the man immediately. For a brief moment, she was transported back to the café where they had eaten *croque madames* and the apartment where they had spent the entire weekend in bed together. "Rudy? Is that you?" she asked in disbelief.

He let out a short laugh. "It is." He stopped laughing abruptly and looked at her. "I never knew you were a Jew," he said with contempt.

Chloe nodded.

"Eh, it doesn't matter. How have you been?"

She glared at him. "How do you think I've been? I am here, a prisoner in this place. How should I be?"

"I'm sorry, that was rather insensitive of me," he said honestly.

Chloe shrugged and shook her head.

"What can I do? I can get you some extra food if you'd like," Rudy said.

"Of course I would," she admitted.

"I'll be right back."

He walked away and Ida came over to Chloe with a curious expression on her face. "What was that about?" she asked.

"I knew him before the war, we had a moment in time together," Chloe said. A pale pink blush came to her cheeks.

"Oh, well, you have an opportunity with him," Ida said.

"What does that mean?" Chloe asked.

"You can find out what happens to the children. You might even be able to make their lives a little better."

It was as if a bright light suddenly illuminated the darkness in Chloe's heart. "Yes, perhaps you're right. Perhaps I can make a difference."

When Rudy returned a few minutes later, he took a large hunk of bread out of his uniform pocket and handed it to Chloe. She was hungry, starving, but she broke it in half and shared it with Ida. She put her half into her uniform pocket. "Thank you," she said.

"I'll try to bring more tomorrow," Rudy said, almost apologetically.

"Rudy," Chloe said, "may I ask you something?"

"Of course. Go on."

"The children that arrive each day on the transports, what happens to them?"

He looked away. "This is war, Chloe. I have no control over what happens to them."

"I understand. It's not your fault," she managed to say. She asked again nervously, "Please just tell me, what happens to them?"

"You don't want to know."

"I must know."

Rudy cleared his throat. "They are euthanized."

"What do you mean? They are killed?" Chloe said in horror. "I thought they went to a camp for children."

"They are gassed, Chloe. It's best for them. Their parents are probably already dead and if they aren't, they soon will be."

Chloe could not catch her breath. It felt as if she had been punched in the stomach. "You're telling me that all the little ones I have put on that truck each day since I arrived here have been murdered?"

"I told you that you didn't want to know," he growled at her.

Chloe shook her head. "No, no, I can't believe it."

"You knew all along, Chloe. If you didn't, you wouldn't have asked me."

She realized that Rudy was right. She had known, even if she had lied to herself; deep in her heart, she knew. Chloe turned away. She couldn't look at him. If she did, she was afraid she would beat him with her fists and she knew she must remember that he was, after all, an SS officer.

"I'm sorry," he said sincerely. "I'll do what I can to make things easier for you here, but this is just the way things are. Neither you nor I have any power to change it. All I'm doing is following orders, so the best I can do is bring you and your friend more bread tomorrow. That's all I'm able to do."

Ida, who had been listening, walked over and said, "Thank you. We both appreciate it."

Chloe couldn't eat the bread. It stuck in her throat. When the children arrived on the next transport, she tore the bread into as many pieces as she could and split it among them. She wept as they laid their little heads on her shoulders and lap, and she sang the old, familiar lullaby. As she watched the truck pull away filled with the tiny innocent souls, Chloe wanted to cry out to God for justice, but she didn't. Instead, she began to form a plan, a way to steal a few of the children from the jaws of death and protect them until she could find a way to smuggle them out.

True to his word, Rudy brought bread for Chloe and Ida the following day. But now he wanted more. He suggested that Chloe come to his office at the end of the workday right after roll call. She had come to hate him, but she knew that he had some power to help her save the children. Chloe would sacrifice what remained of her dignity if she could keep a precious life from being cruelly taken.

FIFTY-SIX

That night, Chloe went to Rudy's office. He was waiting for her with bread, cheese, and a fresh orange, which was usually impossible to get.

"I brought you a feast," he said, smiling. "Eat, please."

She wanted to pack the food up and take it to the children the following day, but she knew that would displease him. If he was displeased, he might stop bringing the extra bread, so she sat down and ate. Her immense hunger took over and she gobbled the food until she almost vomited. After she had eaten, Chloe looked at him and asked, "What do you want from me, Rudy?"

"Come on, Chloe. You're smarter than that. I think you know what I want."

She nodded. He could do whatever he wished with her, and she would have no recourse. "I'll give you what you want if you'll help me," she said.

He looked at her, puzzled. "I could take whatever I wish from you, Chloe. Don't forget who I am and, more importantly, who you are."

"I know, but I also know the real you, Rudy. You are a gentleman. You are the kind of man who only wants a woman that wants him, too. There's not much fun in it otherwise, is there?"

He shrugged. "I suppose that's true. So, what do you want? More food? A different job? To work in the kitchen perhaps?"

"No," she said. Chloe began to unbutton the shirt of her uniform, revealing her breasts. "I want you to help me hide a few children from each transport until we can get them out of here. In turn, I will fulfill every fantasy you have ever had."

A wicked smile slowly inched across his face. "You're one cunning little Jewess, aren't you?"

"Will you help me?" she asked.

He laughed. "I've always loved a challenge. I know you hate me now and that makes me want to win you. Ah, Chloe, you are such a delight in my ever-boring world. So, if you can promise me that you will fulfil my every fantasy, no matter how vile you find it to be, I will help you."

Chloe wanted to vomit, but when she thought of the little faces of the children, so scared, so alone, she smiled back at him, her lips trembling. "Yes, every fantasy, Rudy. Whatever you want. But together we must get at least three children out of this place each week. Now I know that you could lie to me. You could tell me that you've gotten them out and then you could murder them, but I choose to believe that you're far too noble a man to do such a thing."

She noticed that when she called him noble, he straightened his back and nodded. *I have no choice but to believe him*, she thought.

FIFTY-SEVEN

The following day it began. Chloe wished she could save them all, but she knew that would be impossible. So, she took the strongest, healthiest children aside and when Rudy arrived with the bread, he took the children with him.

That evening, after Chloe had done Rudy's bidding, which was repugnant to her, he showed her a small shed where he was hiding the children. "I'll send them out in the next garbage pickup. I'll put them under a pile of garbage and tell them that once they are out of the campgrounds they should wait until no one is around and then climb out and run."

A broad smile came over Chloe's face. "Thank you, Rudy," she said, and she was truly grateful.

The garbage pickup came twice per week. Each time, three fortunate children were selected to escape. And every night Chloe lay beside Rudy and fulfilled her promise.

Ida knew everything that Chloe was doing. "I'm very proud you," she said. "I know how hard this must be."

Chloe nodded. "It is, but every child is precious. Every one of these little ones had a mother and a grandmother. Each time I save a life, I think of my own granddaughter, and I pray that somehow she will be saved."

. . .

Rudy and Chloe's arrangement continued through the brutal winter months. Rudy gave Chloe an extra blanket. She was grateful for it, but when one of the young girls in her block was freezing as she was secretly giving birth, Chloe gave it to her.

FIFTY-EIGHT

Finally, spring arrived. Even in the dark corners of Auschwitz, hell on earth, green grass grew, and dandelions shook their golden heads in the wind.

Chloe and Ida were waiting for a transport one afternoon when a new SS officer approached them. "Well, well, if it isn't Chloe Levin," he sneered. "I saw you dance once when I was in Paris. I was with my mother at the time. She really thought you were something to see. After the show, we waited for you to come out and sign an autograph, but you only signed a couple, and you didn't sign her program. If she could only see you now. I wonder what she would think."

Chloe looked away.

"Don't you dare ignore me," he said, twisting her head and hurting her neck.

"I'm sorry," she whispered, wishing he would go away. She was expecting Rudy to arrive at any minute to take the three children who she chose from the transport that was about to arrive. This man's presence was going to get in the way.

"Who knew that under all that talent you were nothing but a lousy Jew?" He laughed. "Now, you'll dance for me like a marionette."

The train whistle blew. Chloe was trembling. Her nerves were on edge.

"Dance, ballerina, dance..." he said, laughing.

Chloe Levin would not let him see her cry. She was terrified of him, but he would never know it.

"Dance for me, ballerina," the SS officer commanded, eyeing her up and down. Her stomach turned.

"Not on your life." Chloe spat the words out.

He laughed. "Have you ever heard the term 'Burn, Witch, Burn!'? Well, if you keep this up, that might just be your fate."

"That's your plan, isn't it? That's what you do to all Jews," Chloe replied sharply, trying to keep her voice even.

"That remains to be seen."

Rudy finally arrived. He stared at Chloe then he turned to the other officer. "I'll take this from here," he said.

"Be careful, Ostendorff. You show far too much sensitivity towards these Jews. If you keep it up, it might cost you your career."

Rudy Ostendorff glared at him. "I am your superior officer. If you speak that way to me again, it might just cost you your life."

FIFTY-NINE

Ruth had trained Mimi to determine whether a stone was real or fake, and to decipher real gold from brass. She was also a good friend. Sometimes when they were cleaning the display cases and they had a moment to speak, Ruth told Mimi how much she missed her sons and her husband. "They were all arrested before me. I have no idea where they are. I don't even know if they're alive."

"I miss my husband and my grandmother more than I can ever express. Now that I know I'll never see my husband again, I feel miserable all the time," Mimi said.

"I've told you before, you must try not to think about it. I know it's hard. Believe me, I know. But you cannot allow yourself to dwell on this."

"Do you think we'll ever get out of here?" Mimi asked her friend.

"I don't know. I've heard so many terrible stories about some of the other places where they're keeping prisoners. It is not as bad here. I've heard that people are starving and freezing to death. So, I try to look on the bright side and say to myself that at least we have some food, not the best perhaps, but some. And we have shelter. Besides that, it seems that so long as we follow their rules, they don't beat us."

"Yes, I suppose you're right," Mimi said. However, she was not grateful to be alive. She was sick over the thought of Michael's death, and constantly worried about her grandmother.

"Stop wasting time talking over there," one of the Jewish guards said sternly. He often took charge of their department when the Germans were busy. "A shipment arrived this morning. You need to get to work sorting through the jewelry. Don't be careless. You must make sure you only keep the quality pieces, no costume junk. As you go through it, put the necklaces in one pile, earrings in another, and so on. Once you've finished, make room in the display cases for the new merchandise."

Ruth nodded. She and Mimi went over to the boxes that had been delivered to follow his instructions.

"Don't look over there. One of the Germans is watching us," Ruth said. "I'm pretty sure it's the fellow who made this delivery this morning. He's probably checking to see if we're going to steal anything. Be very careful."

Mimi nodded, focusing on polishing a silver necklace that had tarnished. She knew she would be in trouble if it was not perfect before it was put on display. "They always think we're going to steal this stuff. What would we do with it anyway? It's not as if we're going to be wearing it. We certainly won't be dressing up to go out."

Ruth smiled. "That's true, but they know that there are things here we could sell for a lot of money. That money could help to buy our freedom, so they're always watching."

Mimi finished polishing the necklace and began to dig through the rest of the box when she stabbed her finger with a pin that was attached to a brooch. She yelped and the guards turned to look. "I'm sorry. I stuck my finger," she said, quickly lifting the brooch to show them. But when the light hit the brooch and the gold shimmered and the stones sparkled, Mimi felt as if she might faint. There was no mistaking it, this was *Bubbie's* brooch.

How did they get their hands on this? she wondered. *Bubbie would never have given it to them. This is the brooch my bubbie gave my mother at the train station the last time she saw her on the morning she left to go to America,* Mimi realized. *Gloria brought it back to her and I wore it to my first dance. The dance where I met Michael.*

Mimi's hands were trembling as tiny drops of blood fell on the brooch. She put it on the side near a pile of other brooches, but she couldn't take her eyes off it.

"What's wrong?" Ruth asked. "Why are you looking at that piece so intently?"

"It's my grandmother's," Mimi whispered.

"Are you sure?"

"I'm sure, but I can't figure out how it got here. She would never have allowed them to take it from her."

Ruth squeezed Mimi's hand. "Oh, Mimi, I'm so sorry."

"I don't understand. Why are you sorry?"

Ruth looked away.

"Tell me, please?"

"These pieces are taken when their owners arrive at the camps. Usually, it means that the owners are dead."

"What are you saying?" Mimi asked, shaking.

"I'm saying that all the valuables we are sorting, and the ones that are here in this store, were stolen from Jews that the Nazis murdered."

"You're telling me that my *bubbie* is dead?" Mimi choked on the words.

"Yes, I think so. I'm sorry. I'm so sorry," Ruth said.

"I don't believe it. I refuse to believe it. Recently someone came in here and told me that they saw my husband murdered. Now you are telling me that my *bubbie* is probably dead, too. It's not possible." Mimi could hardly breathe. "If by some miracle I survive this place, I'll find my grandmother again."

Ruth looked at Mimi with pity in her eyes.

"What's going on here? Why are you talking? You know better," one of the Germans in charge of the jewelry department said as he walked over to them. "There is to be no talking. It slows up the work and there's far too much that needs to be done. Get this shipment sorted now. *Mach schnell!*"

Mimi sorted through the jewelry in robotic fashion, but tears ran down her cheeks. No one noticed except Ruth.

At noon, all the Germans went into their dining room to eat. The Jewish guard in charge had developed a relationship with one of the Jewish women and the two of them crept off into a small private area.

Ruth was busy showing diamond engagement rings to a young man in a Nazi uniform. As Mimi began to arrange the newly arrived jewelry in one of the display cases, she looked around. No one was watching. With trembling hands, she slipped the brooch into the pocket of her uniform.

With all the guards at lunch Mimi quickly walked up the stairs to her dorm to hide the brooch, when heavy footsteps echoed behind her. Before she could turn around, a powerful hand clamped down on her arm like a vice.

He spun her around and she came face to face with a young Nazi—one of the delivery drivers who brought the merchandise each week. "I was right. It's you," he said. His voice was low, almost a whisper.

Mimi felt terror seep into her bones as she cast her eyes to the floor. *Did he see me steal the brooch?*

SIXTY

As Friedrich was a staunch supporter of the Nazi party and he had been generous with donations, after a while, he was able to secure Nick a job that was less intense than his previous work. Nick was assigned a position driving a truck. Sometimes he was responsible for delivering stolen artwork to Switzerland. At other times he was in charge of driving a special prisoner to one of the camps, but mostly he picked up valuable items that had been stolen from prisoners at Auschwitz and other camps and then brought them to the Levitan department store.

He knew that the crates in the back of his truck contained the possessions of those who had been murdered in the gas chambers and then burned in the crematoriums. Although he hated to think about it, he was glad that at least he was not expected to do the actual killings.

Sometimes when Nick arrived at the gate in front of Auschwitz, he would look up and see the ever-present sign that read:

ARBEIT MACHT FREI

"Work Makes One Free." *Lies*, he would think, *the Nazis are nothing but liars and murderers.* He was ashamed of himself, ashamed at how powerless he had let himself become. The guard at the gate who he had come to know would nod, and Nick would try to put the troubling thoughts out of his mind as he drove inside. He took the shortest route possible to the area that the prisoners called Kanada. He wanted to see as little of the prisoners in Auschwitz as possible.

Kanada was the place where boxes would be waiting for him. As soon as he arrived, several prisoners would load the stolen goods into the back of his truck, then he would leave and begin the long drive to Paris to deliver them to the department store. He drove out of Auschwitz as quickly as he could and kept his eyes on the road in front of him. He dared not look around because he knew that there were piles of dead bodies stacked up everywhere, waiting for their turn to be burned in the crematorium.

Sometimes when he got out of his truck the crematoriums were working at full speed and the ashes from the burnt bodies fell on the shoulders of his uniform. On those days, Nick could not eat. But Auschwitz had a sickly smell that permeated the air every day. Sometimes when the wind was blowing in a particular direction and the stench was too much to bear, Nick had to pull his truck over to the side of the road after he left the camp and vomit.

A year or so after Nick started driving the truck he was given several days off. Since his leave was a surprise, he hadn't had a chance to let his parents know he was coming to stay, but he was glad to have the time away from work and to be able to enjoy home comforts for a week.

Nick was excited to see his mother and she was equally glad to see him. Gloria hugged him and he almost broke down in tears. Sometimes he felt like he was losing his mind. It was hard to explain his feelings, but everything he had seen had left an indelible mark on his soul. Nick felt damaged and dirty.

He no longer enjoyed attending political meetings and avoided them whenever possible. Even though he appeared to be doing alright on the surface, he wasn't. During many nights he had terrible haunting dreams of the face of the baby he had been forced to shoot at Babi Yar.

Sometimes in these nightmares he saw piles of dead bodies. Other times he didn't see bodies, but he heard people's screams. He would wake in a cold sweat, afraid to go back to sleep and see the dead who would return to haunt him. Deep purple circles formed under his eyes, and he was shocked to see the gaunt reflection staring back at him when he looked in the mirror.

Nick began to realize that Friedrich would go out at night and not return until the following day, and he noticed that his father and mother did not sleep in the same bedroom anymore. It dawned on him that Friedrich was unfaithful to his mother. He wanted to ask his mother what had happened and when things had gone sour, but he couldn't find the words to ask her.

Gloria pretended not to notice or care that Friedrich was so clearly disinterested in her, but Nick knew his mother better than anyone else and when he looked closely at her, he could see the pain behind her forced smiles. He began to resent Friedrich for the way he was mistreating his mother.

Friedrich was a weak man who had been spoiled and pampered throughout his life. Unlike Gloria, who had struggled, everything had been handed to Friedrich. It was easy for Friedrich to love the Nazi Party. He had never experienced the brutality of battle, and he had never been forced to murder innocent people. He just sat in his comfortable home and created unrealistic ideals in his mind.

As Nick and Friedrich grew more distant from each other, the admiration Nick had once had for Friedrich faded away. At first, Nick was hurt by the loss of the relationship between himself and his father. But instead of dwelling on what was missing in his life, he spent his entire visit with his mother. As they walked the grounds of their home together each morning, he was reminded of how he had felt when he was a boy and he and his mother were by themselves. At night, alone in his room, Nick would stare at the ceiling and thoughts of Mimi would flood his mind. Her sparkly blue eyes, the way she would throw her head back and giggle. The thought of Mimi made Nick smile. But then his smile broke and it felt as though a spike had gone through his heart.

Friedrich was so determined for me to stay away from Mimi, and I blindly listened to him, Nick thought, filled with regret. *Why? Because she is Jewish? I ignored her letters, and I treated her so poorly. I let Friedrich fill my heart with hatred that was based on a lie.*

A week later, Nick returned to work from his leave. His superior officer seemed to like him because Nick did as he was told and never complained. Although Nick secretly hated the Nazi Party, he allowed his superior officer to befriend him. Nick knew that he might need this man's help someday and so he respected the gesture of friendship.

"Welcome back." His superior officer greeted him with a smile and a handshake.

"Thank you, sir." Nick returned the smile.

"Did you have a nice visit?"

"Yes, it was very nice," Nick replied. He decided it was best to keep his family's personal business to himself.

"Can you come into my office for a few minutes before you begin your work today? I'd like to speak with you," the officer asked.

"Yes, sir," Nick said. He followed his superior officer into the office.

"I want to talk to you about something that's rather personal, but I feel it's important."

Nick was concerned about what he might say, but he just nodded in agreement.

"I'm going to speak candidly. I think that's the best way for us to approach this."

"Yes, sir."

"I've been giving it a lot of thought, and I think it would be beneficial if you were to get married. You're old enough to be settled down, and a good solid marriage to the right girl will help you in your career," he said earnestly.

Nick breathed a sigh of relief. He was glad that they were not going to discuss his father's infidelities. He had been given this advice about marriage many times before. "I've considered marriage, but I never seem to meet the right girl for me," he admitted.

His superior officer laughed. "Ah, all of that stuff about love and romance is nonsense. When you turn off the lights, they're all the same in the dark. I've been married three times, to three beautiful women, and I'll tell you what I've learned. I've learned that it's easy to find pretty ones, but the best thing to do is find a girl that is passive. One that never argues with you. If you can find a girl like that, it makes your life far easier."

Nick managed to force a smile. "I'm not ready to get married," he said, wondering what had inspired this conversation.

"If you're afraid you'll lose your freedom to be with other women, take it from me, you won't. At least, you certainly don't have to. If I were you, I'd get married for my career. Besides that, it's nice to have a wife at home who cooks for you and cleans your house. If you need a bit on the side, well, why not?"

Nick thought about his mother and how hurt she looked under her smile. He remembered the trembling of her hands when Friedrich said he was going out for the night and might not be home until the following day. Although he didn't want to explain his feelings to his superior officer, he knew that if he ever got married, he would want things to be right.

Nick never wanted to be unfaithful. He could never put a woman through the things Friedrich was putting his mother through, but he didn't want to explain. He just smiled at his superior officer and said, "I'll try harder to find the right girl."

"Also, I see you've grown a beard," his superior officer said. "I strongly suggest you shave that as soon as possible. Beards are frowned upon. Besides, it covers your entire face. You're a handsome man, why would you want to wear a beard?"

"I thought it looked good," Nick lied. The truth was, he'd grown a beard because without it he felt vulnerable.

"Well, shave, will you?"

"Yes, of course, sir," Nick said, but he planned to keep the beard for as long as possible.

SIXTY-ONE

Mimi put her hand into the pocket of her uniform and felt the cold metal of the brooch.

A young guard marched over to Mimi, shoving the delivery driver out of the way. "Why is your hand in your pocket? What do you have in there?"

The guard turned his attention to the driver and said, "You have to watch these Jews. They'll steal anything they can get their dirty little hands on. Although"—the guard winked at the driver—"this one's unusual: she's actually rather pretty. It's lunchtime and everyone is busy, so if we had a mind to, you and I could take her upstairs to the floor where we sell the beds and have a good time with her. There's no one up there right now."

Mimi felt a cold chill running down her back. "No!" She felt like she was going to scream but her voice came out as a quiet croak.

The men ignored her for a moment. They were looking at each other and assessing the situation, and then the guard said, "Come here, girl. Let me see what you have in your pocket."

Mimi wanted to run away but there was nowhere to go or hide. She knew that when the guard found the brooch, he was going to punish her for taking it.

She stood frozen, unable to move.

Run, Mimi thought, as her heart beat like a tiny bird in her chest. But there was no place to run to. Her feet felt as though they were welded to the floor.

The guard's thick, hairy hand entered the pocket she had sewn into her uniform. He laughed as he removed the brooch. "I knew it," he said.

The room went dark. Mimi was dizzy and felt as if she might faint.

"Would you look at this?" the guard said to the truck driver. "I knew she was stealing something." He hesitated and then a wide sneer spread over his face. "So, before we punish her, shall we take her upstairs and have some fun?"

The guard stuffed the brooch into his uniform pocket and put his gun to Mimi's back. "Walk," he said and led her to the stairs. The driver followed. With his gun planted firmly into the small of her back, the guard forced Mimi to climb up two flights of stairs before they reached the sales floor where the mattresses and beds were sold.

The driver followed quickly behind them.

Since the store was closed for lunch, the mattress area was empty. The guard pushed Mimi onto a bed and immediately began to undo his pants. Mimi covered her eyes. Tears were streaming down her cheeks, but she dared not scream. If anyone caught this guard raping her, he would tell them about the brooch and then they would kill her anyway.

As long as she was alive, there was a chance she might make him pity her and let her go once he was done with her. There was no doubt in her mind that this massive hairy man was going to rape her, and she was going to have to endure this. "Please, please don't," she begged. "How would you feel if someone did this to your sister or your mother?"

"Shut up," the guard said, but he didn't seem fazed by her question. He looked at her and laughed as he pulled the skirt of her uniform up to her waist. Mimi turned her face away in shame.

She felt the muscles inside of her womanhood clenching in protest. Without thinking, she reacted by pushing her skirt back down to cover herself. This angered the guard.

"I'm losing my patience with you," he said as he slapped her across the face.

Mimi could feel a scream rising in her throat, but she bit her lip to stifle it. *Maybe I should scream? That would make him kill me,* she thought. *I have nothing left to live for anyway. My husband is dead. My dear bubbie is probably gone, too. Perhaps it's best if I just start screaming and he ends this nightmare for me here and now.*

Suddenly, a loud gunshot followed by the acrid smell of gunpowder stunned Mimi. For a moment she thought that she had been shot, but the guard collapsed on top of her, and she felt his warm blood oozing on to her neck and chest.

The driver lifted the guard up and threw him off Mimi. She scrambled to her feet, bile rising in her throat as she grabbed the brooch from inside the dead man's pocket. Her eyes darted frantically. *What if the other guards in their lunchroom had heard the gunshot?*

"Don't worry," the driver said quickly. It was as if he had heard her thoughts. "The rest of the guards wouldn't hear the gunshot. They're drinking beer and eating. They don't want to be bothered. Besides, their lunchroom is several floors down from here. I've dined with them, and they get quite loud once they start drinking. But we don't have much time."

The driver began to pull one of the mattresses over to where the body lay on the floor. Mimi rushed over to help him. They placed the mattress over the body, covering it and the pool of blood. "They won't find him for a while," the driver said.

Mimi glanced up at the driver. He was tall and even though he wore a full beard, she could see that he was handsome. She didn't know why he was trying to help her, but she was grateful. There was something about his eyes that was strangely familiar.

She couldn't explain how she had found the courage to take the brooch from the dead guard with this man watching her. She was shaking, unsure of why she felt like she could trust him. *What was it about him that made him stand up for her when he was a Nazi and she was a Jew?*

There was a softness in his eyes, a kindness when he looked at her. His lips trembled. *He looks so familiar, yet I can't really see his face,* Mimi thought. *He's covered in hair with that beard.*

"You don't recognize me, do you?" he whispered.

"I don't know. You look familiar to me. But..." she said nervously as she wiped away the blood that had sprayed on her lips. She looked down at the guard and remembered how serious this situation was. "He's dead."

"Yes," the handsome and mysterious driver said, "he's dead. You don't have to be afraid of him anymore."

"There are more guards here, lots of them, and when they see thi—"

"Is your name Mimi?" He cut her off mid-sentence.

She nodded. "Yes, how do you know my name? Everyone here is referred to by a number."

"Mimi, it's me... Nick," he whispered, his eyes locked into hers. "Mimi, look at me. Do you remember me now?"

She stared at him. Her eyes grew wide. He was older and his face had matured, but his eyes... his eyes were the same. *Could it really be him?*

She began to cry. "Nick..." Mimi could barely breathe his name. He was one of them; she recoiled. Her mind swarmed with a mixture of emotions.

"You've changed so much. You're taller and you have a beard! Is it really you?"

Nick smiled shyly. "Yes, it's really me. I grew up. I'm not a boy anymore. You've grown up, too." He reached up and touched his beard. "By the way, they hate it."

"Who hates it?" Mimi could not believe that he was standing in front of her.

"My superior officers. They hate my facial hair. They want me to shave it." Nick ran his hand over his thick beard.

For a moment, they stood staring at each other and then Mimi looked down at the pool of blood on the floor and at the brooch in her hand. "We have to get away from here," Nick said hurriedly, touching her shoulder and locking his eyes on hers.

At first, she flinched. Being touched by another man, let alone a man in a Nazi uniform, sent a chill down her spine. But Mimi's eyes met Nick's, and she was suddenly transported back to when they were children and the way he had always protected her. "I'm a Jew, and no matter what happens, if it's bad, they'll think I am responsible for it and I'll be punished. I must go back to the jewelry floor now and pray they don't find out that I was involved in this."

Nick shook his head. "No, Mimi, don't go. I'm not going to let them hurt you. I'm going to get you out of this place."

"Are you crazy? If they find out what you did, you'll be in plenty of trouble as it is. I suggest you get back in your truck and get out of here as fast as you can."

"No, I'm not leaving you behind. We're going to go downstairs to the floor that has women's clothes. You're going to change and put on a regular dress. As long as you're not wearing that uniform, no one will even suspect that you're a Jewess. Then we'll take a few things that we'll need to escape from this place. We'll leave here together, Mimi, me and you." He paused, looking at her. "It's a good thing that they decided to put you here in the department store instead of in one of the camps. As you still have your hair, it will be far easier to disguise you."

Mimi stared at him. "But, Nick, I'm afraid," she whispered.

"You can't stay here. It's too dangerous. You're going to have to trust me, Mimi." Nick cleared his throat. "Do you remember how you trusted me when we were children?"

She smiled at the memory.

"I always took care of you, Mimi. I'll take care of you now if you'll allow me to."

Mimi nodded. In a small voice, she said, "I trust you, Nick, I trust you."

"Good," he answered quickly, patting her shoulder. "Now, hurry, come with me."

As the store was closed to the public for lunch, the guards were all still eating their lunches and drinking beer in one of the rooms upstairs. Nick and Mimi went down the stairs to the floor that held women's clothing. She knew the consequences of getting caught, so she was trembling as he selected a plain, dark-blue dress that looked like it would fit her. Then he helped her to try on shoes until she found a pair of low-heeled pumps.

"Put these on quickly," Nick said, whispering. "I don't think anyone will see the dead guard or notice that you're gone for several hours, but even so, the sooner we leave this place the better. I'd like to put as much distance between us and this store as possible."

Mimi nodded.

"I'm going down to the men's floor. We'll need boots. I can get them there. Wait here," he said.

"Nick, don't leave me."

"I'll only be gone for a few minutes."

She nodded.

He raced down the stairs to the floor where the men's clothes were sold. There he grabbed two pairs of pants and two shirts in his size. Nick then searched until he located the smallest pair of men's pants he could find, along with a shirt, two warm coats, two pairs of socks, and two pairs of work boots—one for him and another for Mimi.

These were things they would need if they were going to make it through to the mountains. Nick put everything into a duffel bag that he had found along with several things they might need for first aid. Once the bag was packed, he headed back to the women's clothing floor where he had left Mimi.

Mimi changed her clothes. She thought of Ruth and wished she could help her, too, but she knew that Nick was taking a risk as it was, and she couldn't ask him to take her friend as well. It was already going to be difficult for two people to escape without being seen. She said a prayer for her friends at the store, and then she reached into the pocket of her uniform and grabbed the brooch. The brooch that meant so much to her and her *bubbie*. The brooch that had paid for her passage to Europe when her parents had died. The brooch that had in some miraculous way found its way back to her. She held it tightly. *Mama, Bubbie, I love you both.*

She hid her uniform that was covered in the guard's blood under a pile of dresses that had just arrived. As Nick hurried back into the room, Mimi released her golden blonde hair which fell to her shoulders in waves. Nick stared at her for a moment in awe of how beautiful she was. She saw him watching her and smiled nervously before quickly braiding her hair and tying it with a white ribbon she had found in one of the display cases.

"Mimi, you are beautiful," he said softly. "In fact, with your blonde hair, you look like the perfect Aryan girlfriend for a Nazi officer. Come on, let's go, give me your hand. We should hurry."

As Nick took her hand in his, Mimi was transported back to childhood and the moment when he had held her hand as they walked up to the door of her *bubbie's* apartment for the first time.

A tear fell down her cheek when she thought of her beloved grandmother, but she didn't stop to wipe it away, there was no time for sentiment. *Not now.* Mimi steeled herself and followed Nick to the stairs and then out the door at the back of the building where the boxes were unloaded. Nick checked to make sure that no one was out there. It was early afternoon and sometimes the guards finished working after lunch. They would let the Jewish kapos handle the prisoners. He hoped that would be the case today.

Nick took a deep breath and sighed. "At least the loading dock is empty."

Mimi asked, "Should I hide in the back of the truck?"

"No, get into the cab and sit beside me. We're going to hide you in plain sight. I know several of the guards at the checkpoints. They consider themselves my friends. So, when we see them, I'll tell them that you're my girlfriend and you're accompanying me on my drive today. They won't think anything of it because of the way you're dressed. The ones who don't know me will believe me, too, because of your blonde hair and blue eyes."

Mimi nodded. "Nick, I really hope this works."

"It will, it has to." He smiled, but she could see his hand trembling on the wheel.

As Nick began to drive, Mimi felt a lump in her throat as she remembered how hurt she had been when he severed their friendship. She tried to banish the thought from her mind. He was helping her to escape now, but the memory was gnawing at her, and she had to know why he had never answered her letter. *What if I was wrong? Perhaps he never received my letter. Perhaps he had not stopped caring about me.* "Nick? I must ask you something," she said.

Nick looked over at her. "Yes?"

"Why are you doing this? Why are you putting yourself and your job at risk for me?"

For several long moments he didn't answer and then he said, "It's a long story, but I'll tell you if you want to know."

"I do want to know," Mimi replied.

He nodded. The sun had just begun to set and it was growing dark. As they drove through Paris, he told her everything that happened at Babi Yar and how he had lost his faith in Hitler and the Nazi Party.

Tears rolled down Nick's cheeks as he confessed to the murder of innocent people while he had been following orders. "I thought I might be able to kill in battle although I never relished the idea, but I never thought I could kill women and children." He was choking on his words, but he dared not stop the truck for a minute. They had to get out of Paris before the guards began to look for Mimi. Nick cleared his throat and then continued, "I killed innocent people. They forced me to do it, but I should have been brave enough to refuse and accept the consequences. I did eventually, but not before doing something I can never forgive myself for." He looked away from Mimi. "Please don't ask me what I did. I can't bear to tell you."

"They would have killed you if you didn't cooperate?" Mimi asked.

"Yes, possibly. At first, I was afraid to stand up to them, but then I just couldn't do it anymore. My stepfather thinks that I'm weak and an embarrassment to our family. Since that day, I realized that the whole Nazi Party and everything it stands for is evil. That's why it was easy for me to shoot that guard."

Mimi listened quietly until he had finished his entire story. She remained silent, but she reached over and took his hand and gently squeezed it.

He squeezed her hand back and said, "I hate Friedrich, my adopted father. He's still very much part of the Nazi Party. I wasn't paying attention before, but the last time I went to see my family I realized that he's unfaithful to my mother. I saw how much pain it causes her, and I can never forgive him."

Mimi nodded. Several moments passed then she asked, "But, Nick, why didn't you answer my letter?"

Nick hesitated for several moments and then said, "Friedrich poisoned my mind about you and your grandmother. He told me to stay away; I was a foolish child, so I listened. I knew you liked me, and I didn't want to lead you on. You were so young and I was already a teenager. I didn't know what to say to you, so I didn't write." He cleared his throat. "I was wrong to do that, and I'm sorry, Mimi."

She thought about telling him how hurt she had been, but they had a long journey ahead of them and she decided to let it go.

Nick stopped the truck in front of a general store where he went in and purchased food and water that he packed in the duffel bag. He returned to the truck and they continued on their way.

He had been right. It was easy for Nick to get through the checkpoints in his Nazi uniform. Most of the guards knew him because he had been making this trip at least once a week for a few years now. Only one of the guards asked him who Mimi was. Nick didn't get nervous, he just smiled and explained as casually as he could that Mimi was his girlfriend. The guard didn't ask any other questions and to his relief no one asked to see Mimi's papers.

They drove through the night without resting. As the city disappeared behind them, giving way to the beautiful French countryside, they continued on their long journey. They passed farms and small villages, and day turned to night again. They were both exhausted, but they were in a hurry to put distance between themselves and the guard who lay dead under a mattress at the department store.

By afternoon the following day, weary and badly in need of rest, Mimi and Nick arrived at the foot of the Alps. "We're going to have to leave the truck here. I'll hide it from the street. We can't take it any further, the terrain won't allow us to. We must go the rest of the way on foot," he said. "I know you're tired—I'm tired, too—but do you think you can make it?"

Mimi nodded.

"Good," he said. "Put on the pants, shirt, coat, and boots that I brought for you. I'll go behind that tree over there and change out of this uniform. The sooner we can cross the border into Switzerland, the better."

It was a difficult climb, especially since they were both so tired, but Nick took Mimi's hand and helped her as they hiked the treacherous ground until darkness fell. "We have to stop, we both need to rest," he said. "Besides, I don't know these mountains well enough to navigate them in the dark."

"Have you been here before?" she asked.

"Once, with my adopted father. But it was many years ago."

She nodded. "I've never been here."

"Switzerland is beautiful. I think you'll like it. We're going to try to get to Bern. We should be safe there."

"I'm sure I'll like it. You don't know how much I appreciate you helping me like this. I never thought I would escape. I was certain that I was going to die in that store," Mimi said.

Nick smiled. "There's always been something special between us, Mimi."

"Yes, that's true."

"Even when we were just little children," he said, taking a hunk of bread out of the duffel bag, tearing it, and handing her half. "Can you ever forgive me for not answering your letter?" he asked.

Mimi shrugged. "I was very hurt. Devastated, in fact."

"I know and I'm sorry. I can't change the past. But can you try to forgive me?"

"I already have, Nick."

They ate in silence for a few minutes and then Nick said, "I was floundering before I saw you again."

She didn't say a word. It was a starry night, and his eyes twinkled in the light of the stars.

He said, "I dated plenty of girls. I was trying to find someone who I wanted to spend the rest of my life with, but they all fell short. I didn't think I'd ever marry. Then there you were and everything made sense. Suddenly I understood why none of the other girls had ever been right for me."

"Nick." She said his name softly.

"My heart was always searching for you, but I didn't know it until I found you." He leaned over and kissed Mimi.

A single tear ran down her cheek. "I was married. My husband died. He was murdered. But..." Her voice caught in her throat. "But I never stopped having feelings for you, Nick. You were always someone special to me even though I never thought we would meet again."

He touched her cheek. "But here we are," he said. "It feels like it was always written in the stars, doesn't it?"

"Yes. It does," she agreed.

"When we get to Bern, I'll find a forger and have papers made for you that say you're a Christian. That should keep you safe. We can get married, if you'll have me?" he said nervously.

They were both silent for a moment. Nick touched her hand. "Mimi, what do you say? Will you marry me?"

"Nick." Mimi paused. "Yes, Nick, my answer is yes."

He took her in his arms and kissed her. Mimi felt warm and safe for the first time since she had been separated from her family. For the first time in a long time, she felt like she had come home.

After a few minutes of silence, she asked, "Will we stay in Bern? What about your mother?"

"For now, yes. When this is over, if it's ever over, we'll return home so I can tell my mother what happened."

"I don't know if my *bubbie* is alive, but as soon as it's safe, I must try to find her."

"We will. I promise we will try."

EPILOGUE
1944

Mimi and Nick were married at the courthouse in a civil ceremony on a cold winter day in Bern, Switzerland. There was no fancy wedding and no guests to invite, but they were happy to be together and to be alive.

They had found freedom to live without fear, and in safety, and they had found each other. Nick had saved some money, but not much. Mimi offered to sell the brooch, but he refused. "We'll be alright. I'll find a job and we'll be fine. That brooch is all you have left that belonged to your mother and grandmother. If we have to sell it, we will. But I'll do everything I can to prevent that from happening."

After a long search for housing that they could afford, the couple moved into an inexpensive apartment. Nick found a job in construction close by. And in a remote area, in a private ceremony between himself and Mimi that summer, he burned his Nazi uniform. In 1945, on a sunny day early in the morning, Mimi gave birth to a beautiful baby boy who they named Laurence for her mother.

. . .

Once the war finally ended with Hitler's defeat, Nick sat down and wrote a letter to his mother.

Dearest Mother,

I should have written to you long before this, but since the Germans censored the mail, I was afraid it might not be safe for you. I'm sure you spent endless days worrying about me and I'm sorry if I caused you distress.

Let me explain what happened. As you know, I became very disenchanted with the Nazi Party and one day when I was making a delivery to a department store, I saw Mimi. She was a prisoner and working for the Nazi Party as forced labor. The minute I saw her again, I knew I had to help her escape. I'll spare you the details, but we had a harrowing escape to Switzerland where we are currently living with our son. Yes, Mother, you have a grandson! It would bring both Mimi and I great joy if you would come to visit us. I have missed you terribly and I know you would love our little boy. However, please do not bring Friedrich with you as I would rather not see him again. I know he only tried to do what he thought was right, but Mother, he was wrong. He was so wrong and if I had listened to him, Mimi might not have survived the war.

Mimi and I have so many memories of you. The other night we were talking about our voyage when you took us across the ocean. We were so little and she was so scared, but she still remembers how kind you were to her. She says she loved you like a second mother. Please know that we think of you often. Mimi and I both send you our love and we are eagerly awaiting a response from you. We can't wait to see you again.

Your loving son, Nick

Nick mailed the letter. Two weeks passed before he received an answer to his correspondence. It came in the form of a very formal letter from Friedrich telling him that his mother had died a year ago. There was no explanation of how or why she had passed on. Although Nick would never have returned home even if Friedrich had asked him to, Friedrich did not invite him to come back to Berlin. The tone of the letter was cold, except for a very strange paragraph:

Nick, I was glad to see that you know that I did the best I could raising you. I think you made a mistake marrying a Jewess, but you are the only son I have ever known. Although I would prefer you do not return to Berlin, I will always regard you as my boy. My only boy.

Nick showed Mimi the letter. He was heartbroken at the loss of his mother, and he wept in Mimi's arms that night. She wished she could comfort him, but there was nothing she could do other than hold him and tell him that she loved him. The war had taken so much from everyone.

In 1947, Mimi, Nick and their son returned to France to search for Mimi's *bubbie*. They returned to the apartment where Chloe had lived, but found that there was a new tenant. Mimi took a bus to the ballet studio, but it had become a restaurant.

Nick suggested that they search the displaced persons' camps where they left a forwarding address with the Red Cross. They searched many displaced persons' camps in France, Germany, and Poland.

The devastation Hitler had caused across Europe was horrifying. So many people were dead and so many others were missing. Cities had been destroyed by bombing. Nick couldn't wait to leave, but Mimi begged him to give her more time and so they went to the Red Cross, hoping to get help in locating a missing person.

However, there was no information anywhere about her grandmother. It broke Mimi's heart. It was as if her wonderful grandmother had never lived at all. The Nazis had wiped her off the face of the earth. But Mimi knew that even if she couldn't find her *bubbie*, her *bubbie* would live forever in her heart.

After an exhaustive but unproductive search the family returned home to Bern.

Twelve years passed during which Mimi had two miscarriages, but she finally gave birth to a second child. This time it was a girl. She considered naming her Chloe for her grandmother, but since Jews only name for the dead and she still held out hope that her grandmother might somehow be alive, they decided to name the baby Gloria for Nick's mother.

A year after the birth of her second child, Mimi was knitting a blanket when a letter arrived at her apartment. The children were playing; she could hear their laughter in the other room as she tore open the envelope.

The letter was in German. It was from a woman who said she got Mimi's name and address from the Red Cross. The letter explained that she had known Chloe. They had met in Auschwitz.

Mimi felt her heart flutter as she sat down on the sofa and continued to read. The letter explained that the woman was writing because she and Chloe had promised each other that if one of them survived and the other didn't, the survivor would find and contact the other one's family. Mimi felt her heart drop. This meant that she must stop holding out hope.

With trembling hands, Mimi turned to the second page of the letter. It read:

Your grandmother was an extraordinary woman. She cared about other people so much that she was not content to save only herself.

She was a hero, Mimi. Your bubbie died trying to smuggle children out of the camp.

You see, she and I were responsible for rounding up the children when they first arrived. We were expected to keep them calm while waiting for a truck that was to take them to a place for children only. Your grandmother and I were led to believe that the children would be safe in this place, but we discovered that this was another Nazi lie. When your grandmother found out that the Nazis were taking these little ones and killing them, she went crazy. She didn't care about her own safety anymore. She began trying to hide as many children as she could when they arrived.

At night, she loaded the children into the back of garbage trucks and hid them under piles of trash. She saved countless young lives. However, she was caught by the guards one night and the next day she was punished by death.

I am so sorry to have to tell you this, but she made me promise that I would find you and tell you so you wouldn't spend your life searching for her. I know this news comes as a terrible and hurtful shock, but you must never forget that although she perished under the Nazi regime, your bubbie was a true heroine. You should be proud to have been her granddaughter.

May God bless you and your family.

Ida Rosensweig

When Nick returned home from work that evening, Mimi let him read the letter. After he finished, he took her into his arms and held her tight.

Mimi was haunted by memories of her grandmother. It constantly bothered her, knowing that the Nazis had obliterated her grandmother from existence. As it stood, there was no grave to visit, no trace at all of her *bubbie*. So she began to write down everything she could remember about her grandmother—every memory and every story that her grandmother had ever told her.

Mimi spent hours racking her brain trying to recall everything she could about her *bubbie's* life. For a full three years she wrote, often staying awake all night until she felt as if she had written every detail she could recall. Then she went to Nick and said, "I need a favor from you. I know how hard you work, and I know you've been saving for us to buy a home, but I need to use some of the money."

"Of course, darling, but what do you need it for?" Nick asked.

"I must go to Israel."

"To where?"

"To Israel."

"That's very far, Mimi," he said, genuinely concerned. "I don't think it's a good idea."

"Nick, please listen to me. I heard about the Holocaust Remembrance Center that was built there and I must go."

"Why?"

"I've been writing my *bubbie's* life story and I can't let go of her without knowing that her memory will be preserved. So I've decided that I want to ask the people at the museum if they will put my *bubbie's* brooch on display there alongside her life story. This way, she will be remembered forever. Everyone who goes to the museum will know her again and she will live forever in our hearts."

"Oh, Mimi," Nick said, taking her in his arms. "You need to do this, don't you?"

She nodded. "I do. I need it more than I can express."

Nick adored Mimi and he indulged her whenever possible, so he agreed. But even with all that he had saved, there was not enough money for the entire family to make the trip, so Mimi made plans to go alone. Nick was very worried about her, but he knew he had to let her do it.

Two weeks later a certified letter arrived for Nick; it was from an attorney in Germany. His mouth fell open when he read the news that Friedrich had passed away, leaving his entire estate to Nick, his only surviving relative.

"Mimi," he called out. "Mimi, come here!"

Hearing the urgency in his voice, she rushed into the living room from the kitchen where she had been preparing dinner. "What is it, Nick?"

"We're wealthy, Mimi. Friedrich has passed away and left his estate to me."

She could barely speak.

"We'll have to go to Berlin and settle things, but I think I'd like to sell the house and live here. After what the Germans did to the Jewish people, I can't see how we could live in Germany."

Mimi nodded.

"We'll go as soon as we all return from Israel," he said. "Now we have enough money for all of us to go there."

She turned away from him. "No, Nick. It will be too traumatic for the children. I want to do this alone."

"Are you sure, Mimi?"

"I am," she replied.

A month later, Mimi boarded a ship and traveled to Israel. Although the accommodation on the ship was rough, she didn't care. Mimi was on her way to the Jewish homeland, the perfect place to lay her grandmother to rest. She arrived at the port exhausted but ready to complete her journey, and made her way to Yad Vashem, the Holocaust Remembrance Center.

When Mimi arrived at the museum, she asked to speak with a director and was taken to an office at the back of the museum. Her hands trembled as she waited, holding the large document she had written about her grandmother.

It was only a few minutes before a middle-aged woman with kind eyes came out of the back room. "I'm Devorah Kleinstein," she said. "I heard you were waiting to speak to me. How can I help you?"

"My name is Mimi," she said in her most professional voice, and then she explained why she had come. "My grandmother was murdered in Auschwitz. There's no evidence that she ever lived and I just can't let the Nazis wipe her memory from the world." Tears fell from her face. "I want to leave this brooch and this hand-written book about her life here because I was hoping you would put these things in one of the display cases. This brooch is worth a lot of money and, believe me, my husband and I have needed this money many times, but I refused to sell it. I couldn't part with it that way. It's worth more than money to me. There's a story behind it and the story is in this manuscript. I want to put both the brooch and the book in a secure place here at the museum where I know it will be safe, and it will be seen by young people who need to know about what happened to us Jews during the war."

Mrs. Kleinstein nodded. "I understand. You want the world to know that your grandmother lived."

"Yes. Not only did she live, but she was a hero. She saved children. Besides that, I want to be sure that what was done to our people is never forgotten."

"Before I can agree to put this in the exhibition, I must read it."

"I understand."

"May I take the manuscript?" Mrs. Kleinstein asked gently.

"Of course," Mimi said, handing her the pile of papers.

"Where are you staying?"

"At a hotel not too far from here."

"Leave me a phone number where you can be reached and I'll call you as soon as I finish reading it. I'm sure you must understand that I have to read the entire book before I can allow it to be displayed here in the museum."

"Of course, I do. I'll wait at the hotel to hear from you," Mimi said as she placed the brooch down on the table.

"Take the brooch with you. I don't want you to leave it here until I know whether we can do this."

. . .

A couple of days later, Mimi received a call from Mrs. Kleinstein. "The book was wonderful, and we would be honored to exhibit this book and the brooch as your grandmother's legacy."

"I'll bring the brooch to you this afternoon," Mimi said. "If that's alright?"

"Yes, of course it is. I'll be waiting for you."

Mrs. Kleinstein allowed Mimi to lay the book and the brooch side by side in a glass case and then she locked it. Mimi turned to her and said, "Can I have a minute alone to say goodbye to my *bubbie*? There's no grave site, so I must say goodbye here."

Mrs. Kleinstein nodded. "I'll leave you alone," she whispered and then she squeezed Mimi's shoulder.

Once Mrs. Kleinstein had gone, Mimi closed her eyes and found that it was easy to envision her grandmother's kind face. "I miss you so much, *Bubbie*," she said aloud, hoping her grandmother could hear her somehow. "If we had to say goodbye, I wish it had been in person, but this is the best I could do. I will always love you. You were there for me when I was just a little girl and my parents both died. I remember the day I first met you. I was still reeling from the loss, and I thought my whole world was ending, but you gave me a reason to live, a reason to go on. Now I'm hoping that this display with your pin and your book will share your memories with the rest of the world." Tears streamed down Mimi's cheeks. She bit her lip and then she heard it distinctly: her grandmother's voice. Her *bubbie* was speaking to her in her mind.

"Don't cry, my little one. I'm always with you in spirit. So, I'm going to tell you the same thing I told your mother that day she and I had to say goodbye on the dock when she was leaving for America. I put my brooch in her hand, and I said, 'Keep this for me until we meet again.' And now I say to you, I'm glad that you have found a home for the brooch where the world will know our story through it. Mimi, go on with your life, raise your two beautiful children to be kind and loving people. Nick is a good man. He loves you. Go home and be happy, be healthy, and until we meet again, just know that I love you..."

"*Bubbie*," Mimi whispered, "you will never be forgotten."

A LETTER FROM THE AUTHOR

I always enjoy hearing from my readers, and your thoughts about my work are very important to me. If you enjoyed *Until We Meet Again*, please consider telling your friends and posting a short review. Word of mouth is an author's best friend. To hear all about my releases with Storm publishing, you can sign up here!

www.stormpublishing.co/roberta-kagan

Also, it would be my honor to have you join my personal mailing list. As my gift to you for joining, you will receive three free short stories and my USA Today award-winning novella complimentary in your email! You can sign up here: www.robertakagan.com

You can review my book on Amazon!

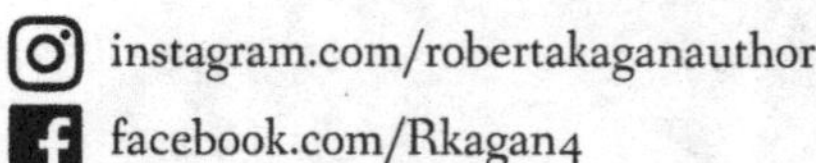

instagram.com/robertakaganauthor

facebook.com/Rkagan4

ACKNOWLEDGEMENTS

I would like to extend my deepest gratitude to Claire, Oliver, Lucy, Amanda, and the entire Storm Publishing team. Your unwavering dedication, creativity, and hard work have brought so much care and brilliance to this series. I feel truly fortunate to be surrounded by such a talented and supportive group, whose passion and commitment have helped shape these books into what they are today. Thank you for believing in me.